# The Lady's Sweet Revenge

## SAFELY IN SCOTLAND, BOOK 3

# ALLISON B. HANSON

## ARE YOU SIGNED UP FOR DRAGONBLADE'S BLOG?

You'll get the latest news and information on exclusive giveaways, exclusive excerpts, coming releases, sales, free books, cover reveals and more.

Check out our complete list of authors, too!

No spam, no junk. That's a promise!

### Sign Up Here

www.dragonbladepublishing.com

*Dearest Reader;*

*Thank you for your support of a small press. At Dragonblade Publishing, we strive to bring you the highest quality Historical Romance from some of the best authors in the business. Without your support, there is no 'us', so we sincerely hope you adore these stories and find some new favorite authors along the way.*

*Happy Reading!*

*CEO, Dragonblade Publishing*

# Chapter One



*May 1815, The Coast of Scotland*

BLINKING INTO THE darkness, Harlow Haverston tested the binds on her wrists. As her hands were tied in front of her, it was easy work to reach up and remove the sodden gag from her mouth.

Despite her throbbing head, a painful reminder of the earlier attack, she focused on what to do next. It took another few moments for Harlow to realize the swaying beneath her was not caused by dizziness, but that she was in the holds of a ship. The groaning of the vessel and slapping of waves against the hull proved her theory correct.

Hearing footsteps above her, she resisted the urge to scream out for help. No doubt everyone aboard was well aware she was there and had assisted in her capture. There would be no help found here.

It had seemed like no less than forty men had overpowered her uncle and their groom before pulling her from her horse. One moment they'd been riding in a secluded area in Hyde Park, enjoying the early morning sun before the heat of the late May afternoon chased them indoors. The next moment, they were overrun by bandits and she was knocked over the head and dragged away.

She shivered, despite the muggy warmth of the room she was

in. It would be an easy thing to give into panic. She didn't know why they had taken her, what they planned to do with her, or even where she was or where they were taking her.

"Focus on what you can control," she said aloud, quietly. Hearing the shaky quality of her voice shamed her even if no one was there to hear it but her. She was a Haverston, and Haverstons didn't crumble into a fit of tears.

Or at least that is what her brothers—all five of them—always told her anytime her lip began to tremble with the slightest hint of imminent tears.

But she had to think even her sturdy older brothers would be just as frightened and worried in this situation. She wished even one of them was with her now. Or Uncle Edgar. What had happened to him after she'd lost consciousness?

Uncle Edgar, her mother's younger brother, had always been more like another brother, not that she'd needed another. But he was doting and kind while her brothers, protective as they were, often tried to do things without her.

She'd been determined to follow them wherever they went. Their constant challenges had gotten her into plenty of scrapes as a girl. Though nothing as serious as the one she was in now.

Her mother and father, the Duke and Duchess of Ardmere, must be beside themselves with worry. Being the youngest and a daughter, Harlow was often treated as something of a princess by her parents, which often gave her brothers more reason to keep her out of their mischief.

She always seemed to be caught in the middle. Not strong enough to keep up with her brothers, but too strong-willed to be coddled by her loving parents.

And now, it seemed, all her attempts to find a place she fit in had been nothing but a waste of her time, for she was going to die at sea.

But as she sat up, allowing her head a moment to right itself, she was determined not to let that happen. Besides, if they'd wanted her dead, there would be no reason to take her with them. They could have simply done away with her in the park and avoided all the extra effort of kidnapping her.

A cold thought wound through her throbbing head. She swallowed, trying to keep from being ill. For the fact they'd taken her could mean she faced an even worse fate than death.

For now, she was alone in this room, still intact as best she could determine. The only pain came from her head in the place where they'd struck her.

These ravenous barbarians she'd created in her mind, based on the quick glimpses she'd had of the men who'd pulled her from her horse, must have had orders to deliver her unharmed. For it didn't seem likely men like that would have much by way of patience.

Which meant, according to all she knew about kidnappings from reading Theodore Stonecliff novels, they needed her alive for their purposes.

Her father, the Duke of Ardmere, was among the richest men of the ton. A fact Harlow attributed as the reason she'd not yet wed at five and twenty. The sizeable dowry her father offered attracted the worst fortune hunters in Society. Fortunately, her brothers were able to tell her who was and was not acceptable. So far, in these last eight years of dancing with every marriageable man in London, none of them had gotten the approval of her brothers.

She could almost laugh at how little it mattered that Lord Resch didn't own enough horses, or how Lord Wenwrike slurped his tea. She should have married by now.

The offers had become fewer each year as she got older and less desirable, according to the ton. And now she would be ruined if anyone found out about this. Being ripped from her horse in the park and put aboard a ship with no chaperone.

She would likely be ransomed for a hefty sum. And her father would pay it without batting an eye, the sooner to have her back home. The useless princess, saved by her father's fortune.

"No," she whispered as her fingers clenched into fists. She

would need to do better. She needed to get free before her father had to part with so much as a shilling for her return. And once she did, she would accept the next offer of marriage she received, regardless of what her brothers thought of him.

She could very well die on this ship not ever knowing the touch of a man, but, by God, if she lived she would find out. She only needed to escape this godforsaken ship.

But how?

Growing up with so many brothers, they had often spent their summers in the country playing bandits and highwaymen. She, being the only female, was always set as the hapless victim. Of course, escape hadn't been her biggest concern because they were her brothers and meant her no harm. Usually. She did remember one such time they had left her tied to a tree and then the call from the kitchen of warm pies caused a distraction that left her stuck there for more than an hour.

She'd found a sharp rock on the ground and had all but worked her way through the ropes when they finally returned—Thomas, the youngest brother, with blackberry jam still on his face—to cut her loose. They'd praised her on her skills in escaping and the six of them had spent the rest of the afternoon devising ways to get out of certain knots.

The next day their attentions had drifted to something else. Harlow shook her head wishing they'd spent more time practicing and embracing such a skill since it would be quite useful to her now.

There would be no sharp rocks about, but if she could find something else she might remove her bindings as it was just her wrists, not her whole body like it had been during the blackberry pie abandonment.

Looking around the room she was in, she cursed. It was too dark to see anything but a sliver of light she guessed came from the bottom of a door.

Unable to see, she could almost feel the darkness closing in. She squeezed her eyes shut despite it making no difference and focused on taking deep breaths to calm herself and think.

She breathed in the salty air of the ocean, mixed with the musty undertones of wet wood. The scents of lamp oil and smoke combined with the remaining threads of rosewater and horse coming from the riding habit she still wore.

Lamp oil. At first she thought of it as a way to light the room so she might see, but then she thought of another option. If there were a lamp in the room, it would mean she likely had access to a glass globe.

With her hands out in front of her she scooted off the edge of the bed and found her way to the wall, noticing then her boots were gone, leaving her only in stockinged feet. Keeping her shoulder against the wall to help with balance as the ship swayed and lurched, she shuffled her feet with her hands out in front of her searching for something. Anything.

When she reached a wall within a few steps she realized the room she was in was quite small, which sent another wash of panic through her. But she forced herself to keep moving until she came to a stand of some sort with a shallow lip, maybe to keep things from rolling off the surface during high seas.

Groping across the stand she found what she determined was a metal pitcher. Turning it about, her fingers met nothing but smooth surfaces. She moved on, feeling nothing else.

A whimper escaped as failure grasped her lungs. She could not give up.

She thought of her room at home to calm her. She spent hours in the light-blue haven, reading of adventures she wished to go on someday. She wasn't sure if it was the fear or the blow to the head that kept her thoughts sloshing about in the same way as the sea outside the ship, but she couldn't seem to focus on one thing.

It was as she was chastising herself on distractions of travels to China that she considered something quite important while also completely unrelated. Wall sconces.

Still hovering next to the stand with the pitcher she reached up above her on the wall and was greeted first with a metal bracket and then with the sleek coolness of a glass globe.

Heavy footsteps caused her to freeze in place as her heart pounded. She couldn't be stopped when she was so close to finding a way to escape her binds.

The shadow moved across the sliver of light at the bottom of the door as the footsteps faded. The person had passed by.

Working more quickly now, she twisted the globe free and as she raised it to smash it against the edge of the stand, she paused, thinking of the danger.

Breaking the globe in such a fashion would scatter shards everywhere. She could step on a piece and cut herself. It would be more difficult to hide if she was tracking blood. Not to mention the noise might bring someone to investigate.

Holding the globe against her chest, she braced her shoulder against the wall to return to the bed. Wrapping the globe inside the bedspread, folded double to muffle the sound, she bashed it with the pitcher.

Where she'd hoped for the soft crash of glass, she heard only a loud thump. Or perhaps it felt loud in the small confines of the silent room.

With more strength each time, she tried three more times before the glass finally broke.

She smiled at the clinking sound as she splayed the blanket out. There was no other option but to gingerly reach across the fragments to select a piece she could use to cut her ropes.

Feeling the burn of a slice on her middle finger and then her thumb, she pressed her lips together and continued until she found a piece big enough for what she needed.

It took precious minutes for her to find the best way to hold the glass so she might work it over the ropes. Frustrated with the slowness, she felt tears prick smartly in her eyes. Had she thought this would be easy? It was nearly impossible to hold the glass in the proper direction.

With each passing second, she worried someone would come

to find her.

Eventually, she felt the rope give way and she was able to work a hand out. She left the rope attached to the other wrist, not willing to spare another minute on it. With her hands free she could move more easily.

Something else had happened as she'd focused on her task. The sky had lightened slightly, casting the room in the smallest gray glow coming from a tiny round window high on the wall.

She could just make out the frame of the door. As she moved forward, she realized she had not considered the possibility that the door would be locked. She almost expected it to be when she reached for the latch, but it opened and the door swung in easily enough.

She silently praised her captor's underestimation of her. They, like most men, probably thought she would wake screaming and be unable to do anything else but curl into a ball in a pile of hearty burgundy wool and tears.

After checking to make sure no one was close by, she slipped into the narrow corridor and squinted at the warm glow of the wall sconces lighting the path. Picking the opposite direction from the hull of the ship, she slowly worked her way toward the steep stairs.

On deck, she saw a few men working at the far end of the ship. Glad for her dark clothing and hair, she rose out of the stairs and scurried for the shadows away from the men.

She stumbled over something but covered her mouth to keep from crying out in pain. Giving her foot a moment to recover, she kept moving but froze beside a dinghy as voices came closer.

"…much farther do we have to go?" one man asked. "Seems a waste to go all this way just to turn back to return her to her father and collect our pay."

The other man chuckled. "Nay, we don't plan to return her. Cap'n said Polk is lettin' us keep 'er. The toff didn't put up much ov'a fight to protect his poor niece when we took her. Stood there, 'e did."

"Do ye think Polk will give the cap what he wants now?"

"I 'ave my doubts as he didn't stop us. But if not, 'tis no matter. For once the Zephyr is safely ported in Inverness, a ransom letter will be sent. Ye know Cap'n Merrick wouldn't take a job without a weighty payout." The two laughed.

"What if they don't pay?"

The man chuckled again and the sound sent a shiver up Harlow's spine.

"They will pay. And we get to keep the girl to do what we…"

Harlow swallowed and shrunk back closer to the edge of the ship as the men passed, their horrid conversation getting pulled away by the wind.

Polk. They'd spoken the name as that of an accomplice. Someone who had been aware of the activities in the park, and had no intentions of returning her to her father even if he paid the ransom for her safe return.

They'd said he'd not tried to save his niece. Which meant there could be no misunderstanding that the Polk they spoke of was her Uncle Edgar Polk.

Swallowing too loudly, she shuddered with the betrayal that her dear uncle would be part of such a plan. Her mother's younger brother had always doted on her and her brothers, almost seeming like another sibling rather than an uncle.

How could it be that someone she loved so dearly planned to trade her off to these men and whatever abysmal fate they had planned for her? They spoke of him giving something to the captain; she imagined him getting himself into debt with such people and couldn't fathom it. She'd not known her uncle to be a heavy gambler. Had he borrowed the money and been unable to pay it back? But why would her uncle ever have need to borrow from brigands such as these? Her father would have helped him.

Whatever the reason, she wasn't going to puzzle it out here.

In a daze, she glanced over the deck of the ship. It would soon be light, taking the safety of the shadows with the sunrise. She would be found missing from the room below and they would begin searching.

Looking over the rail at the black water below, she pulled away. She was a fair swimmer, but had only ever done so at the lake at Haverston Manor. She'd never tried to swim in the ocean. And how far would she have to swim?

She frowned at the dingy. If she could deploy it she'd be able to row to safety. But she knew she was not strong enough to do so and even if she could, it would be far too noisy and take much too long.

She had this one chance of escape and she wouldn't waste it. If she were going to have to swim, she didn't want the hindrance of yards of heavy wool weighting her down. She deftly removed her riding habit, and then reached behind her tugging at the laces to remove the corset that would restrict her movement. It was unladylike to be sure, but she'd rather not drown if it could be helped. Propriety easily fell victim to survival.

Reaching inside the small boat, she gripped onto an oar which was tangled in a fishing net attached to odd chunks of wood. Rather than spend more time disentangling the net, she just grabbed onto the whole mess and tossed it over the edge of the ship a few seconds before she crawled to the rail.

"If this doesn't work, at least I'll be dead and won't have to worry over whatever fate I would face here." As motivational speeches went, she found hers quite lacking, but it was the best she could muster before jumping into the inky depths below and letting the sea take her.

$$\text{—} \cdot \text{—} \textit{✦} \text{—} \cdot \text{—}$$

# Chapter Two

STEPPING OUT OF the castle, Reese Maclanahan, Earl of Breckenridge, took a deep breath of salty, morning air and felt all his worries melt away. Perhaps that was an overestimation. A large portion of his worries melted away, some were stuck fast and never seemed to budge.

Since he'd only arrived home to Slains Castle late last night, he was hopeful the remaining concerns would scatter with a brisk walk on the beach escorted by the only female he knew could be trusted.

"Belle, get out of there," he called to the deerhound who had been eager to have her master home until she caught sight of a hare in the brush. With a sniff, the large, gray dog shook her shaggy coat and came lumbering back to his side.

He smiled up at the blue sky. It would be a warm day, even if the morning still carried a bit of a chill. He loved being home in Scotland over the busyness of London.

As they carefully traversed the steps down to the shore, Reese frowned at the slight ache in his leg. While his injury was nearly a year old, and he no longer walked with a limp, it was a frequent reminder of how close he'd come to never seeing the sight of the ocean breaking itself on the rocky shore again.

Even his closest friends didn't know what had truly happened. He was forced to lie and say he'd been thrown from his horse. Such was the life of an agent of the Home Office. Which was why he'd given it up this season.

A man became too cautious once he'd faced such danger and barely walked away.

He looked around now for a different type of danger in the form of some young lady ready to catch him in a compromising situation.

He'd been lucky to have escaped London without a wife after the last trap had nearly succeeded. He'd not been prepared for his own mother to play a role in his demise.

Of course, she'd said it was for his own good, and the chit, a Miss Agatha Renway, was from one of the most noble families, or perhaps it had been that her bloodline could be traced back centuries, or mayhap even that her teeth were in good repair. He couldn't rightly remember as he'd set his staff to packing immediately, so he could leave.

It was one thing to have to navigate the desperate mamas who hoisted their girls on any man with a title and two coins to rub together. But to have his own mother be a part of the treachery was too much.

He may have gone to one of his other country homes that were closer, but he'd always felt at home here at what seemed like the edge of the earth. He'd spent most of his youth at Slains until he'd gone off to school in Edinburgh. But that was not the reason he chose this home from the others for his escape.

No, it was because his mother—an Englishwoman through and through—hated Scotland for having had to live here with the auld earl for far too long. She'd vowed never to return after his father had died six years ago.

*Never* still seemed like too soon to have to see his mother, the traitor, again. He knew he'd forgive her eventually, but some time apart was appreciated.

On the beach, Belle came rushing up with a stick almost as long as her body. Using his foot to break the limb into a more manageable piece, Reese gave it a great throw at the edge of the surf and smiled as Belle took off after it. The dog deftly maneuvered the rocky shore before she jumped into the waves to retrieve it and brought it back so he might do it again.

She would be content for him to do it all day long, and at the moment he didn't think he would mind so much. Throwing a stick for his beast of a dog gave him time to sulk.

It wasn't only his mother's duplicity that had him leaving London in such a rush. It was different being in town for the Season without the excitement of his more important work. It was one thing to attend a ball as a reason to gain access to Lord Ruston's study so he might get a look at his ledgers and report back to the Home Office, yet another to attend only to dance and partake in watered-down lemonade while evading the plethora of debutantes chasing him.

While that was part of the reason he'd not enjoyed himself, he had to admit there was yet another, more personal, cause of his hasty retreat.

He was lonely. His best friends had stayed in the country this year with their families.

There were plenty of men that would have welcomed him at their gaming tables or shared a bottle of whisky. But after spending time with his friends and their newfound happiness in the most conventional of places, Reese had conceded his fight to remain a bachelor. He'd even gone so far as to ask a lady he'd taken a liking to for her hand.

And she'd said no.

*No.* To him. An earl, and one of the richest men in the entire kingdom. Miss Sheridan had passed on his proposal so she might marry a second son of a baron. Reese wanted to be a better man and wish her every happiness, and in truth, he did. But it seemed especially painful after all his reluctance to be married that the time he'd given into a brief display of emotions and actually asked someone to marry him, he'd been rejected.

Now, with the sea air filling his head, he could see what a

boon it had been that she'd refused him so she might instead have a love match. He'd been in a low place, missing his friends, which had apparently caused some sort of temporary madness. He was glad now, though the wound still stung when he recalled her look of pity.

It figured the one woman he might have considered seemed to be the only unmarried lady in London not attempting to dig her claws into his flesh.

"You are a loyal girl," he said to Belle as she brought the stick back and beat him about the legs with her large, soggy tail.

He tossed the stick as far as he could down the beach and watched as she ran after it, and then past it to a large lump lying in the sand.

"Belle! Belle, come here at once!" he called and then picked up his pace when she didn't pay him any heed. "Don't ye dare eat whatever it is you've found. You do remember what happened the last time." But, of course, she didn't listen as she began snuffling around the thing and barking. "You were sick for days," he said, as if he could remind the dog of what came from bad decisions.

When he got closer, he heard the dog whining as she nosed the lump. At least she wasn't eating it. But then he noticed the lump was a mound of light fabric, and a few steps later he saw a pale, slender arm.

"Dear God," he whispered as he ran forward. Her hair was black as midnight and he remembered the stories when he'd been a lad about kelpies. Beings that wore the skin of a seal while in the water, but could remove it to walk upon land to lure a man to the depths.

He shook his head, thinking he may have gotten the kelpie tale mixed up with that of a siren or a mermaid. It didn't matter. She obviously had legs for they were exposed and he took note of her small, stockinged feet.

For a fraction of a moment Reese wondered if this was yet another trap to compromise him into marriage, but if it were, it was surely a dire one.

Belle whined again and licked the woman's fingers. The woman groaned softly, which allowed Reese to let loose the breath he'd been holding. He'd not wanted to touch her for fear she were dead. He'd been unfortunate to find one of their agents after his death, and the memory of the man's cold skin still haunted him.

The woman moaned a little louder as Reese knelt beside her. She was on her back with the weight of her hair covering her face. He thought she might be better able to breathe if he got the mass of inky tendrils out of the way. Pushing it back from her face, his breath caught when he stared down at her. She was beautiful. Possibly the most beautiful woman he'd ever seen. Even in this state with her hair hanging in clumps and her skin pale and chilled.

He didn't think he'd ever seen her before and looking at her clothing told him nothing, for she wore only a cotton shift. Despite its sturdy weight, it was wet and clung to every curve of her body. Curves he, as a gentleman, should not be looking at.

Turning his gaze back to her face, he caught Belle licking the poor woman in the same way she often woke him.

"Belle, nay." He pushed the dog back but she only circled round to the other side to continue her overeager welcome.

The woman's eyes fluttered open, and he was stunned by how green they were.

"Help," she said.

"Aye, of course. Belle, stop licking the poor woman. This is Belle, she's not a danger, just a menace. I'm Reese."

The woman nodded slightly as if she understood what he'd said, and then she leaned over and retched all over his second-best boots.

<hr>

# Chapter Three

Harlow's body hurt everywhere, but her head was, by far, the worst. While the muscles in her arms and legs throbbed with overuse, her head pounded so horribly it made her stomach twist. Every time she attempted to open her eyes, the light made the pain worse, which is something she didn't think was even possible.

She wanted to cry, but it would surely take energy she didn't have at the moment. Her throat burned from the unshed tears and being sick. Lord, had she just gotten sick in front of the man? Reese.

Strange how things like decorum lost their value in the face of desperation. For she didn't care one bit that she was a mess, at least she was an alive mess and that was a blessed discovery. So long as she didn't expire from the sheer pain of her skull splitting in two.

She gave in to fatigue, and allowed herself to rest.

Later, she attempted to open her eyes again and was grateful for the dimness of the room. Even if she didn't know what room she was in. In fact, she didn't remember leaving the beach.

It was warm and dark. That was all she could bring herself to care about. Not until large, brown eyes with rough, gray fur around them took up her vision. Just before a giant tongue lurched out and stroked her entire face in one swipe.

She jolted and screamed.

"Belle, stop that," a man's voice said sternly. Harlow turned quickly to face him, but learned it had been too quickly when the pain in her head rushed back. She squeezed her eyes closed. "Are ye to be sick again?" the man asked with an edge of worry.

"I—I'm not sure," she decided it was best to be honest. She lay back and focused on breathing in and out slowly. While she didn't trust opening her eyes yet, she found her voice, rough as it was. "Where am I?"

"Slains Castle, my home."

That answer didn't tell her much. She'd never heard of the place. But she'd deal with that later. "Who are you?"

"Lord Breckenridge, my lady."

She searched her mind for having heard his name before and eventually recalled him.

"Golden," she said aloud without noticing. Her head was not up for the task of keeping certain things inside it seemed.

"Golden?"

"Your hair," she explained as some niggling voice told her she should not. That she should stop talking.

"Aye. I guess so."

But she knew his hair was blond. That was really all she knew about him. Except that he was completely unsuitable for marriage. Not that he'd asked. Not that many had asked anymore.

"Who are you?" he asked.

She opened her mouth to tell him, but then stopped and just shook her head.

"Good God. Ye've lost your memories," the man, a gentleman, she recalled, said with a Scottish brogue.

She shook her head again and opened her eyes enough to roll them at the man.

"Of course, I know who I am. I just don't wish to tell you," she rather snapped, and then thought that was rude as she most likely had this man to thank for saving her.

"Why not?" he asked, and rude or not, she just wanted him to stop asking questions that tasked her sore head.

"It's not safe," she said as her energies waned from the conversation. It was frustrating. She was not a weak person. She'd had to keep up with her five older brothers or risk being left behind and ignored. She'd never given up. No matter what they did she managed to do it as well, despite being smaller.

But now she could hardly keep her eyes open.

"Why isn't it safe?" he asked.

Rather than answer, she closed her eyes and drifted once again.

"Uncle?" Reese repeated the word she'd whispered as she'd fallen asleep. Was she asking him to find her uncle, or was her uncle the reason she wasn't safe?

Either way he wouldn't go looking for anyone who knew her since he had no clue where to even start. She hadn't lost her memories, but she'd taken an impressive knock to the head. It had taken seven stitches for Mrs. Garrison to close the wound Reese hadn't seen right away because of the darkness of her hair.

He'd asked his maids to clean her up and put her in a clean, dry gown before settling her in the bed. Unfortunately, the women weren't able to move her around very easily in her state. He'd been called upon to help lift her from the tub and place her in the bed in one of the castle's many guest rooms. He'd done his best not to look, but it was impossible not to catch a glimpse of her in his arms as he'd carried her.

And maybe it had been harder than it should have been not to look, but he was a man after all, and she was bonny. And he *had* managed to get by without gawking at her. Surely that was what was important.

He sat in the chair next to her bed reading the latest Theodore Stonecliff novel while Belle laid against the woman on the bed. He'd shooed the dog away a few times but every time he left the room he came back to find her there and had eventually given up.

At some point, he'd taken to reading the story out loud. Either for the woman, or for the dog, he wasn't entirely sure. When he glanced up he found her staring at him with those moss green eyes. Her cheeks were now flushed instead of pale and that simple change had made her even more beautiful.

Clearing his throat, he pushed a smile to his lips.

"Are ye feeling any better? Mrs. Garrison managed to get some willow bark tea in your stomach. She said it should help with the pain."

"I feel somewhat improved. My head is not pounding as if my brain will beat itself out of my skull."

He smiled at her jest as she reached up. He moved closer to stop her hand from touching the wound.

"Be careful. You had a nasty gash on your head. Mrs. Garrison saw to stitching it."

She looked down at herself, likely noticing the much-too-large dressing gown she was wearing. "Please tell me Mrs. Garrison also helped to bathe and dress me?"

"Aye. She did." It was true enough even if he'd left out the part where he'd assisted. That would be for another time when she was much better.

"You said I'm at Slains Castle. That's in?"

"Scotland. Barely. The castle sits on a cliff at the edge of the North Sea. A few hours east of Inverness. Near Aberdeenshire."

"I've come so far…" she whispered. "I must go. Right away." She moved to get out of bed and gasped either from the pain in her head or that of the badly swollen ankle Mrs. Garrison had noted when she'd bathed the lass.

With a groan of irritation she fell back on the bed.

"I'm sorry, but you're not fit for travel to the next room, let alone any great distance. Where did you say you were from?" he asked, hoping she would give him the smallest clue as to who she was.

"I was in London for the Season. I was riding in Hyde Park when…" She shook her head.

"Miss—or is it missus, or lady?"

"Harlow," she answered, but avoided answering the question he'd asked so he might know her marital status or rank.

"You wish me to call you by your Christian name?" He tried again to learn more about who she was. He'd acquired many interrogation techniques during his time as an agent, but she'd not fallen for any of them yet.

"I imagine it's the least of the many unacceptable things that has happened since I was pulled off my horse in London. For I have not yet met Mrs. Garrison, but my guess is she is not so sturdy as to lift a full-grown woman from a bath into a bed." She raised her brow and Reese felt his face heat under her critical gaze. She was a canny lass.

"Very well, Miss Harlow. I planned to apologize for the impropriety when you were feeling more the thing."

"So courteous of you," she said with another roll of her eyes. For someone with a head injury she was surely in possession of the movement of her eyes.

"If you were riding in Hyde Park, however did you come to be on the beach so far north in only your shift?"

Her eyes glistened and she wiped at them quickly as if offended by her own body's functions.

"Are you trustworthy, Lord Breckenridge? I only remember my brothers telling me you were unfit for marriage, but not much else. I must know if your finances are in decline." She looked about the room as if the furniture and the wallpapering might give her some notion as to whether he was wealthy or destitute.

Unfortunately, the castle did not boast the greatest furnishings since his mother didn't bother to update a place she'd promised never to return to. He didn't need the latest fashions when he was in the country and had not updated them either.

"Why do you ask?"

Her eyes narrowed on him.

"If you think I want to know if your coffers are healthy so I might force you to wed me, you are quite wrong. I have no need of your coin."

"Then you, yourself, come from wealth and you think it possible I might try to leverage your safety for money?" His brows rose when she did not deny it. "My, you do think me the worst kind of man." He shook his head. "I'll have you know, your brothers, whoever they might be are quite wrong. I'm most acceptable for marriage. So much so every marriageable miss has gone to great effort to entrap me."

He didn't know why he felt the need to defend himself and his acceptability. He should be glad she found him lacking so as to avoid any ideas she might get about ensnaring him. As compromising situations went, they were knee-deep in one at the moment. Still, it had irked him that she found him unacceptable.

It was not uncommon for the snootiest of the ton to look down on him and his friends as they were Scots and thought of as rough barbarians, ready to feast on the flesh of virgins or some such other ridiculousness. But most were willing to overlook such possibilities if it meant they could latch onto a rich husband with a title who at least knew how to use utensils.

"If it should reduce the damage to your honor, I would tell you that I already know you are not the lowest of men. For I have met the worst of your ilk, and the most horrid of all seems to be my own uncle."

"You mentioned your uncle when you drifted off. Is he your guardian? Are you running from him?"

She let out a breath and looked toward the window where the drapes were pulled to keep out the last of the evening light. Then she looked down at Belle who had rested her head on the woman's lap. Harlow had been running her fingers through

Belle's coarse coat and looked down at her now as if she hadn't realized she'd been petting the animal all this time.

"Very well, I'm not sure yet if it is a mistake to trust you, Lord Breckenridge, but you have done me a kindness by tending to me, despite whatever pleasure you may have gotten from such a thing. If this animal trusts you, I should do so as well."

As a credit to his honor, it was not much, but he was pleased that she was willing to tell him how she came to be here so he could see to sending her back.

But when she opened her mouth and began to tell him the incredulous tale of how she'd ended up in his home, he realized it would not be so easy as sending her back to Mayfair with a wish of good health.

It seemed this woman would need to stay with him for some time. And if he was not very put out by the thought of it, he chose to ignore it.

———⟡———

# Chapter Four

THE MAN, LORD Breckenridge, listened to her horrid story, looking appalled at all the appropriate times, which was to say everything that had happened to her since she'd been riding in the park.

"And you say your Uncle Edgar, a man who has doted on you since you were a lass, is responsible for such a heinous act?" He seemed shocked, but not as if he didn't believe her.

"Yes. I am to understand he has gotten himself into a mess and owes money to this Captain. For what, I can't possibly know as my uncle is not much of a gambler. But the men aboard the Zephyr said my uncle had allowed them to… keep me."

Reese, she remembered he'd told her his name at some point, looked at her with wide eyes.

"Did you say the Zephyr? That was the name of the ship?"

"Yes. Before I jumped overboard, I heard two men talking about the captain's plans."

"The captain?" he said, his voice dropping to a whisper.

"Merrick," she and Reese said at the same time and he near to jumped up from his seat to pace the room with his hands clenched in his thick, blond hair.

"You were aboard Captain Merrick's ship and escaped." It was more a statement of astonishment than a question, yet she answered.

"It was not so difficult. They hadn't even locked me inside the room. They'd only bound my wrists." She couldn't help her tone of disgust. While she was truly grateful for their ineptness, she was rather offended they thought her such an easy captive.

"Are you complaining about the poor job they did of securing you?"

She hadn't meant to make it so obvious. "It was rather insulting to think a woman so incapable of escaping them."

He smiled and it warmed his brown eyes. She couldn't help but smile back. Then she laughed, one chuckle burst free, followed by another until she was caught up in a state of hilarity. Tears gathered at the corners of her eyes and ran down her cheeks, and she couldn't be entirely sure if they weren't from the fear and hurt resurfacing or the laughter that had gripped her.

"I would have loved to have seen the look on Merrick's face when he learned you were not in that room." He bowed from his seat. "I'm honored to make the acquaintance of the lady who bested Merrick and his savages from the Zephyr."

"It sounds as if you know them."

"No. Though I've heard of them." He frowned and it looked as if he rubbed his thigh. "What else did they say?"

"Once they are safe in the port at Inverness, they plan to send a letter of ransom to my father. I don't think the ransom was meant to cover my uncle's debt."

"Merrick is a smuggler. If your uncle is mixed up with him it would not be a gambling debt. Likely something else."

Smuggling? What had her uncle gotten caught up in? How desperate was he to have handed her over to such a fate to save himself? What kind of a man did something like that? She thought she might be sick again, but Reese was speaking.

"Who are your brothers?" he asked, in a way she thought he hoped was cunning. She was nearly as offended as she'd been with her meager constraints on the ship. Did he think her so foolish as to accidentally give away her secret?

She still hadn't told him who she was. What family she was from. It would do little good to escape one kidnapper only to have this man demand his own ransom for her.

Perhaps, though, it was time to tell him all. If she was wrong to trust this man, she would pay dearly for her mistake. But despite having escaped, she would need this man's help to get back home. For she was in Scotland, with no funds and no proper clothes.

She shook her head and then let out a deep breath.

"My father is the Duke of Ardmere."

His eyes went wide again and then he dipped his head in a quick bow.

"Lady Harlow," he addressed her formally.

She waved her hand. There was really no reason to keep with such propriety now. Not when he was currently alone with her while she sat in bed in a voluminous dressing gown.

She didn't say any of that. She certainly didn't need to point out to him how improper all of this was. She cleared her throat to get them back to the matter at hand.

"Whatever reason my uncle owes him this money doesn't matter. This Captain Merrick meant to hold me ransom, but my uncle had no plans to return me home after they received the money from my father."

"Then we need to write to your father straightaway so he knows you are safe and not to pay it. If they were planning to go to Inverness before sending off their letter, ours will surely get there first."

She had not thought that far, but she nodded and moved to get up from the bed. She forgot her blasted ankle yet again and winced.

"Please. Stay there. I will take care of it."

"They may not believe you if it is not in my own hand. Even then I must write something personal so they will know it's only me that could be writing." She bit her lip as she thought on which of her brothers' many secrets to reveal to prove her authenticity.

"Stay where you are. I will bring the writing implements so you can write a missive while staying abed."

"I'm well enough to get up." She hated being treated like a dainty ninny. And it was true she could get up. Walking, however, seemed beyond her at the moment.

"I trust you to know your own reserves, but I would ask you to give it the night, in case you are mistaken. I'd rather not have to carry you about again."

His cheeks turned the slightest shade of pink and she didn't wish to think on what he might be remembering. She'd jumped in the ocean in only her shift. Wet as she was, she imagined the garment was not fit for providing much in the way of protection from his gaze.

Her own cheeks heated and she pushed the thought away. Whatever he may have seen is far better than what future she was sure to have faced by staying on that ship. The time for coyness was past. She needed to focus on survival and justice.

Justice, she found, ran close to the border of revenge. For the more she thought of her uncle's betrayal, the angrier she became.

He must pay for what he'd done. All these years her brothers had told her how unacceptable all the men of the ton were for marriage. But they had not realized the most dangerous viper lived under their very roof.

She'd trusted her brothers to steer her away from rogues and scoundrels, but she'd fallen victim to Uncle Edgar's duplicity. How naïve she'd been. But no more.

She wouldn't trust anyone. She let out a sigh as Reese turned to leave. It seemed she was willing enough to trust the earl.

He had moved for the door and even in the dim light of the room she noted what a striking figure he made. He was taller than even the tallest of her brothers and wider across the shoulders than them as well. His hair was golden as if he was better suited walking about in white robes carrying a harp like so many angels she'd seen painted in a gallery.

But his eyes were not blue, they were dark as night. Nearly

the same color as the pupils. And while his lips were full and presented a perfect bow, there was nothing cherubic about them at all. Instead they looked like they were made for sin.

She cleared her throat though no one was in the room any longer but her and the dog. Belle. She rubbed the beast behind the ears and Belle nuzzled closer to Harlow's leg. It seemed she had made a friend in the animal. And perhaps with the earl as well. He certainly seemed set on helping her with this mess. She would trust him so far as to get off a letter to her father. She didn't have much of a choice.

This was all her uncle's fault. Her heart turned cold as she realized it would not be enough to just keep him from getting his hands on the ransom. No. The man needed to pay dearly for such a hideous betrayal.

⇛⇛⤜⤜⤛

WHEN REESE RETURNED to the room he found the woman glaring at him as if she might be able to strike him dead with just her gaze.

"I hurried as fast as I was able," he said in his defense.

She shook her head, not as if to tell him no, but as if she were shaking herself from some horrible memory.

"No. I'm sorry. I was thinking of Uncle Edgar. How does a man lure his own flesh and blood into such a trap and then not have even the slightest intention to have me returned safely to my family? He'd just given me to them so they might do whatever they wished with me. I may not be worldly in that way, but even a maiden such as I could tell what kinds of things they intended had I not escaped."

Her lip quivered and she bit it, likely to keep from showing any weakness. He'd never met a more formidable woman than Harlow Haverston.

She'd said she was the Duke of Ardmere's daughter. Reese

recalled the man being a stern, older gentleman, but reasonable, as he'd voted with a level head in the House of Lords. He had five sons. The oldest, the Earl of Fletcher, had married and had a few young sons of his own. With plenty of spares, her other brothers were raucous, but not without honor as far as Reese remembered. Much like himself.

He'd not realized the duke had a daughter, but then why would he have since his goal in recent seasons was to avoid anyone's daughter.

As he looked at her he was certain this wasn't her first Season. Or even her second. She was no blushing debutante, but a strong woman.

"I'm surprised I've not met ye in a ballroom," he said curiously.

She cast her glance away. "I've not been in a ballroom in the last two years. My come out… Well, it was certainly active."

"I'm afraid I don't follow."

"I garnered a reputation for refusing a few offers of marriage."

"I wouldn't say that is uncommon. Many women pass over the early offers if they are waiting for one in particular, do they not?" It was not surprising Harlow would be discerning. She seemed to have a steady head on her shoulders.

"Perhaps. Though I wasn't waiting for anyone particular, and it may have been a little more than a few."

He tilted his head, curiosity taking over.

"How many?" he leaned closer and whispered. She did the same to answer.

"Twenty-six."

"Twenty-six offers of marriage in your first season?" he all but shouted in surprise. "Whatever could have been wrong with all of them?"

"That's a fair question. One I have been asking myself again throughout this endeavor. I trusted my brothers to guide me. They assured me they would tell me who would make a proper husband and who would not."

Reese couldn't help it. He laughed.

Her eyes narrowed on him. Of course, a woman as fierce as she wouldn't appreciate his laughing.

"Forgive me, but despite not being a brother myself, I can almost assuredly say that they found no man suitable for their dear sister."

"I should have seen it sooner, I suppose. You must think me a lackwit."

He shook his head and offered his most sincere expression.

"Anyone would be a fool to think you so. You have been incredibly clever in your escape and have kept your wits when many of the lords of the ton would have trembled in such circumstances." Not him, of course. He'd faced danger and death and lived to tell about it. Not that he could tell anyone about it because it had been a secret mission. One he'd never finished, thanks to Captain Merrick.

"The relationships between siblings is quite odd if you consider it," she said. "They were quite horrid to me when I was a little girl. Leaving me to play by myself if I didn't prove myself worthy with impossible feats of loyalty. But then they are so protective as well. I imagined now that we are adults they would have put their foolishness aside to see me happy with someone. But they still toy with me."

He reached out as if to place his hand over hers but pulled back when he remembered it would be inappropriate. Not that his being in the room alone with her wasn't already greatly improper.

"There is great risk when one embarks on finding a suitable partner. I'm sure they only wished to keep you from being hurt. Even the noblest of us can still be an insensitive lout occasionally." How many of those young misses being forced upon him this season had wished for a happy match with a kind man? And he'd run in the opposite direction without giving them a second of his interest or time.

"If I'm able to get back to Mayfair with my reputation intact, I plan to find my own match. Without any comments from them. After all, shouldn't I be responsible for my own happiness?"

"Ye wish to marry?" Reese swallowed, feeling the familiar instinct of flight.

She smiled. "You may relax, my lord. I'm certainly not considering it at the moment. I only meant to say that I have relied too much on others to make decisions for me and my wellbeing. And I plan to put an end to it. I must learn to trust my own judgment."

"If you determine how one might do that, would you mind sharing it with me?"

"I will certainly keep you apprised." She smiled, seeming pleased with her plan.

"The strange thing is that my best friends fairly stumbled into the best of matches with their wives. Lily and Thea were both in a bit of a predicament, and Finn and Shay—that is Ellis—stepped up and offered marriage to save them." He blinked at Harlow who was most assuredly in the same situation.

Perhaps this was his chance to find a bride he would find happiness with. She was certainly beautiful and smart and while her humor was strained at the moment, he'd detected a bit of mirth.

He stepped closer and took her hand.

"Lady Harl—"

"No, please don't."

"You don't even know what I was to say."

"I do. Or rather, I don't wish to."

He let out a breath.

"Did you just sigh in relief?" She frowned. "My, but, I'm glad to have saved you from such a heinous match," she said with a bit of affront.

Rather than try to put her at ease, he decided to share the truth.

"I'm a gentleman and would have done my duty to protect

your honor, but after evading a marriage brought on by honor and duty all season, I guess I am relieved not to be forced into it."

"I would never want a man to feel forced into marriage with me. And I'll not marry someone whose proposal is offered simply for duty."

"You seem angry that I offered and angry that I'm relieved. I'll remind you, you *just* said you planned to marry." It was possible he sounded slightly irritated as well, for he'd tried to do the right thing and she'd not even allowed him to finish.

"Yes, well, I'm rather busy at the moment, my lord. Might we focus on the stopping of my ransom?"

"Yes." He shook his head. Of course, his question was ill-timed. Had Finn and Shay been refused at first? Reese found he was growing rather tired of being rejected. He decided there and then he'd not ask another woman for her hand in marriage unless he was certain of her response. Which would mean knowing the woman quite well beforehand so as to know what she was thinking.

How exactly would he get to know a woman that well with a chaperone about? He shook his head. It was a matter for another day.

"Let's see to the business of a letter to your family to put their minds at ease."

"Yes." She settled the lap desk over her legs and set a piece of paper ready to write. The quill hovered over the page for a few seconds before she lifted her head and looked at him. "I do thank you for your offer, given in protection. It was quite thoughtful, but when I marry it will be because I want to, not because I'm forced into it by my circumstance."

"As you should. Forgive me."

"I could do worse than you, Lord Breckenridge. You have been an honorable man. Now, what do you know about revenge?"

Reese blinked at the quick change in her demeanor and topic.

"Pardon?"

"I do not wish for my uncle to know his caper his up. Do you think it hideous of me that I am set on revenge? I want him to pay dearly for what he's done. To have used me so wretchedly in his scheme. It is worse than anything this Captain Merrick and his crew could have done to me, for they would have only caused harm to my body, and perhaps my spirit. But what Uncle Edgar has done... he has shifted the base of everything I had known. When I'd thought I'd been loved, I had instead been leveraged. And he must pay for the damage he's caused to my heart."

Her eyes glistened, but like before, this brave woman took a slow breath and sat straight and determined. Reese had wanted to ask her if she would aid him in the capture of Captain Merrick. But given everything she'd been through already, he couldn't bring himself to suggest such a thing and add to her burden. But this plot of revenge could be used to serve two purposes. Bring two disreputable traitors to justice at the same time.

He offered a smile. "I have an idea of how we might get you the revenge you seek."

$$\text{Chapter Five}$$

HARLOW WAS INDEED grateful for Lord Breckenridge's honorable offer of marriage. Not that she'd given him a chance to actually offer, for if she had she might have felt forced to accept.

After all, she'd made a pledge to herself on that ship that she would accept the next offer of marriage she received, so she might know a man's touch. It was something she wanted more than anything. Or perhaps not quite as much as seeing her uncle pay for his crimes.

Even with revenge on her mind, there was a part of her that wished she'd allowed Reese to finish his proposal so she might have accepted. For he was striking and kind with a sharp sense of humor. But she'd also promised she wouldn't marry someone out of obligation and how much more obliging must the earl feel than to have to care for a woman who washed ashore? No. That was not the way.

She might not yet know the way, but marriage was not foremost on her mind at the moment. For she had an uncle to torture.

In the end, Harlow wrote a letter to her eldest brother at his home instead of sending a missive directly to her father. Reese said it would allow the information to arrive without the possibility of her uncle intercepting it.

*Dearest Brother,*

She scratched through the salutation and wrote something David was sure to know had come from her.

*Dearest Gravy,*

"Gravy?" Reese asked from where he stood at her shoulder.

"It's a name we called him when we wished to irritate him. We would shout 'Gravy Davy' and he would hate it, though I'm not sure why he took such offense. Gravy is quite delicious. It wasn't nearly as bad as 'James smells like the Thames' or 'Luke-oo is a cuckoo.' Henry and Thomas were generally spared since their names do not easily rhyme with anything vulgar." She scrunched up her nose. Surely she'd be able to think of something now that she was older with a more robust vocabulary. But not now. Revenge.

"Children really are the worst of Society, are they not?" Reese said. "I feel blessed for not having had siblings. I had three great friends at Heriots. And, of course, my size kept most of the boys from pestering me."

He tilted his head to the side. "What names did they call you?"

She laughed. "Nothing clever enough to rhyme with my name, I can tell you that." Without offering more details she went back to her letter.

*Please read this letter entirely before sharing with anyone else. It is of the utmost importance. Not everyone in our family can be trusted.*

*I'm sure by now you have learned I was taken in the park by a pack of brigands and likely fear for my life. I'll assure you I am well, but for a terrible knock to the head and nearly drowning during my escape from a ship carrying me to Scotland.*

She looked up to where Reese was still reading over her shoulder and he gave a nod of approval. It was what he had suggested she tell them first, for her family was likely worried to death.

> *I was found by Lord Breckenridge, and he has offered me refuge here at Slains Castle until I am able to travel. I would ask you to relay this information to mother and father in private. It is imperative that Uncle Edgar not learn of my escape as it is possible he is somehow involved in my kidnapping.*

This was also at the behest of Reese. While she had wanted to tell David to rip the man limb from limb, Reese stated that they didn't have all the facts and that giving one enough rope to hang oneself was sometimes the best tactic. As it seemed Lord Breckenridge—despite not having siblings—was a formidable planner, she'd gone along with it. Besides she felt she'd be better suited to bestow her acts of revenge on the man when they were not in Polite Society. And there seemed to be plenty of room on the estate to hide the blighter's body.

"You have that look again," Reese said with a slight wince. "The one that makes me very glad I wasn't the one who betrayed ye."

"I'm sorry. It just makes me so mad. I think if I stopped being angry I might break down into tears so I will grip hold of my ire and use it to make the man wish he'd never been born."

"Aye. Anger is a good distraction to be sure. Keeps ye from dwelling on what might have happened."

She nodded in agreement. The truth was, she didn't allow herself to travel very far down that trail for she knew what would have surely happened if she'd not gotten off that ship and even the few times she remembered the men talking on the ship gave her a shiver up her spine.

"I was very fortunate. Not only to have escaped the ship but to have washed ashore on your beach. And had such a fine girl find me," she said as she scratched Belle behind the ear where she liked it best.

"I'll remind ye, it wasn't Belle who carried you up to the castle and had to wash his boots."

She felt her cheeks warm with embarrassment.

"I'm sorry."

"Nay, don't worry yourself over it. I'm just making sure you like me better than the dog is all."

Liking Lord Breckenridge didn't seem to be a problem.

She cleared her throat and turned back to the paper to continue her missive to her brother.

> *You should soon receive a request for ransom, but make sure father does not pay it. One, because I am no longer with the kidnapper and two, because he had no intention of returning me home safely even upon payment of the ransom.*
>
> *Please tell everyone else in Society that I fell from my horse in the park and was taken to rest with a relative in Bath so no one will question my absence. There is a second letter enclosed with mine. Keep it until you receive the letter of ransom and then share it with the entire family.*
>
> *I believe Uncle Edgar will offer to come retrieve me in Scotland. If he does, let him come.*

She was likely making the face again as she considered what she might do when he arrived in Scotland. As bloodthirsty as she'd been she realized she wasn't able to cause him physical harm. Not just because it was illegal, but because she didn't think she could carry out such a thing.

She would consider the perfect way to make him pay for what he did. She would have plenty of time while waiting for her letter to arrive and him to come north.

> *I know this all sounds like something from a Theodore Stonecliff novel, but I assure you, it is true.*

"You read Theodore Stonecliff novels?" he asked.

"Yes, and if you think to scold me for reading books more

suited for a man, I'll remind you I have five older brothers and most of what I read is passed to me from them when they've finished with it."

"I was not going to deliver a scold. I would actually say they are suited for women as well as men. After all, Theodore Stonecliff is in fact a woman."

"Why do you think so?" She thought to the stories and the writing style, but had no inkling if this was true.

"I don't think it. I know her. She is married to my dear friend."

"Theodore Stonecliff, a married woman?" She shook her head. "I am not so ninny-headed to believe such a thing. No husband would allow his wife such a freedom. How many times must I remind you of the five older brothers before you realize I'll not be so gullible?"

He chuckled. "Believe me or no, but it's true. I've no reason to mislead ye. It would seem your *five older brothers* have left you quite cynical."

It was true Lord Breckenridge had no reason to mislead her, but she knew well from dealing with her brothers that one did not need a reason to make a jest except for the amusement of it. And perhaps he was correct about her being cynical as well. If only slightly.

His claim seemed almost so unbelievable as to be true, and so far, Lord Breckenridge had not been caught in a lie. She decided to set judgment aside until she'd come to know him better. She would think on the possibility of such a thing later.

> *If you were to have any doubts as to the authenticity of this letter, please recall that I know you were responsible for breaking father's pistol when you dropped it from the attic window. And since you and I were the only ones there, only I know the truth. And now Lord Breckenridge as he is reading over my shoulder, but I will swear him to secrecy as well. By the way, I don't recall why you said he was unsuitable for marriage, he*

*has been most respectable.*

*Your sister,*

*Lo*


"Lo?"

"Apparently it is tiresome for young men to speak two syllable words frequently, so they shorten them to single syllable
words for ease of use. Dave, Hen, Thom. Luke and James
remained Luke and James."

He nodded.

"What happened with the pistol?"

"We were forever stealing them from our father's study to
shoot at things propped on a fence. One particular time he found
it missing before we could sneak back to return it. Father was
livid because… well, it was quite dangerous, but not the most
dangerous thing we'd done."

"Really?" He shook his head. It seemed she made him do that
quite often.

"Anyway, we had planned to toss it from Davey's window,
but he said it would be obvious he had it because it would be
found on the ground outside his window. So he and I went up to
the attic and tossed it out the front of the house to land in the
drive. Where none of our windows faced."

"Quite a brilliant plan."

"There is a reason none of us were maimed or killed, my
lord. We were very clever."

"Deviously so. I will take the truth of the pistol to my grave,
Lady Lo." He smiled. "My, but that is so much easier to say than
Lady Harlow."

She chuckled at his jest, but she also noticed the heat on her
cheeks. She rather liked hearing the shortened name on his lips.
And in his accent. Not that she could say why.

With her letter finished, she passed over the lap desk so Lord
Breckenridge could write the missive that would accompany hers.

She leaned over his shoulder as he had done while he wrote

and noticed how close she was to his neck. She could smell his skin, salty from the sea with a hint of citrus and sunshine, though he'd spent most of the day inside with her.

She shook the silly thought away. What did it matter what the man smelled like or that it was pleasant?

She watched what he wrote and focused on her plot for revenge.

*Greetings,*

*I have some troubling news as I've found your relative on the shore of my estate. She's alive, but has not yet woken. She has quite the injury to her head, you see. I discovered her identity from the locket she was wearing with the seal of the Ardmere dukedom and wrote to you straightaway.*

"You would have fit in well with my brothers, my lord. You pen a compelling letter. It is quite believable."

"The trick to deceit is to follow the truth as closely as ye can. It is less likely you will forget something and get tangled up in the lie."

"I shall have to remember that." She'd also need to remember that this man seemed quite skilled at lying. And apparently she was not as skilled in detecting a trustworthy gentleman from a rotter like her uncle.

She shook the thought away so not to be called out for glaring yet a third time. Leaning closer again, she sniffed the man as he continued writing.

*She is safe and comfortable at my home. Please send for her at Slains Castle near Aberdeenshire.*

*Lord Breckenridge*

"That should lure him here where I might punish him for what he's done," she said and if her laugh sounded a bit evil, well the man didn't call her out for it.

"Aye. That's what you wished, yes?"

"Yes. Now I have time to figure out how I want to punish him."

Something that would surely cause him the same level of pain she'd felt at his betrayal. Something quite heinous indeed.

# Chapter Six

AFTER SITTING WITH Harlow as they'd written their letters, she'd grown tired and Reese left her room to let her rest.

After he'd noticed not only the way her dark lashes rested on her milk and cream cheeks, but the enticing curves of her body, he knew he needed to write to one of his relatives as well.

The only relative he had left. The one who had betrayed him just a few weeks ago at a London ball.

His mother.

For Harlow was not going to be leaving his home for some time and was in need of a chaperone. One that could assure everyone in the ton that she'd been here with Harlow the entire time.

His first choice would have been Lily, the Duchess of Granton, or Theodore Stonecliff herself, Thea Hayes, the Countess Ainsley. But since both were in a family way, thanks to his devilish friends, they would not be up for travel.

He would need to depend on his mother.

It was important that Lady Harlow's reputation remain intact. And not because he didn't want her ruin to be cause for a forced arrangement between them. Or not only for that reason.

Harlow seemed to have had a change in perspective. As many do when they are faced with the possibility of death, she'd looked upon her life and identified those areas where she held regret. Specifically in allowing her brothers to scare her off from any potential match that might have given her happiness.

She now seemed set on righting that wrong, and Reese wanted to see that nothing that happened here in Scotland would put her newfound resolve in jeopardy.

Her brothers could only be pleased that her anger for retribution was focused solely on their uncle rather than them. At least for now. And since Reese had use for this plot to lead to the capture of Captain Merrick, Reese needed Harlow to trust him.

Providing a chaperone seemed like one way to do that.

Besides, his mother owed him a great debt after her diabolical scheme. It was with that thought in mind that he penned a short letter.

*Dear Mother,*

*Please come to Slains Castle forthwith and plan for an extended stay. I appreciate you do not particularly relish returning to Scotland, but your presence here is most important. Know if I do not see you in a fortnight, all funds in London and Sussex will be cut off until your arrival.*

*Breckenridge*

He wondered if it sounded a bit too harsh, but then decided he didn't care.

He had one final letter to write. But this one took much longer for it needed to be encoded for secrecy. It had been some time since he'd needed to employ such a skill, but he managed to convey the message.

*Make haste to the Inverness. Captain Merrick is heading there with the Zephyr.*

Sealing all the letters, he hired a post boy to take them to London as fast as possible. They would surely arrive before Merrick's letter of ransom. Reese assumed the man would still send his demand even when he learned Harlow had jumped overboard. Likely, he would assume she'd drowned and it wouldn't change his plans if she were dead.

Reese had waited a long time to bring Merrick to justice.

Rubbing his thigh where the wound still ached on occasion, Reese remembered the blinding burn when he'd been shot by Merrick. Reese wished he'd be the one to bring Merrick back to London and see him hanged, but he would have to trust the job would be done by the other agents.

Reese sighed. Merrick had been so close to ending him. This time Merrick would be apprehended. And Reese would have to be satisfied with the small part he played in that outcome.

It seemed his guest was right about the cleansing power of vengeance. For Reese felt better already.

He peeked into Harlow's room again to find her still sleeping. Belle raised her head and tilted it to the side as if asking him if it was time to go for a walk. Walking along the beach was the only thing that lured the beast from Harlow's side.

"Keep watch, lass," he told the dog and closed the door feeling unsettled. He found he enjoyed talking with her and when she slept so often, as was expected of someone healing, he didn't know what to do with himself.

When days ago he'd been content to be there alone and read or see to the grounds, now he was wishing Belle's movements would have woken his guest.

"Are you a'right, my lord?" Mrs. Garrison asked as he passed by Harlow's room again.

"Aye. I'm fine."

"Did ye need something?" She looked at him and then looked at the door pointedly.

"Nay. It's just I hadn't seen Belle and wanted to make sure she was in with Lady Harlow." As lies went, this was not the best, but it was the best he could come up with on such short notice. Any proper housekeeper would mind her own business and accept his reasoning with a nod and a wish for a good day. But of course not his housekeeper.

Mrs. Garrison's eyes widened. "If the dog isna at your side, she is surely with the lady. Belle's barely been away from her but to eat her dinner."

"Yes. Well. Now that that's sorted, I'm free to return to my study." Where he should have already been to avoid such a conversation.

"Aye, she'll likely not wake until morn. She needs rest to heal."

Of course, he knew that. He'd just thought as much. He didn't need his housekeeper to explain the way injuries worked. She knew well enough of his experience with such things as she'd been the one to tend to him when he'd been shot.

Instead of arguing, he simply turned and went to his study, closing himself in and taking a deep breath.

"The lass is not for you. She's been through a horrific ordeal and is recovering from an injury. She surely doesn't need you sniffing after her," he said aloud to himself so there could be no mistaking his intensions and what he thought of them. "You are a safe port in a storm. Nothing more."

He went and poured himself a dram of whisky so at least then he'd have a reason to be talking to himself. Thanks to a few too many drinks, it was where he ended up falling asleep, awaking just as dawn approached.

It was too early for her to be awake so he took his time getting dressed and eating. Harlow's breakfast was taken to her room as she was still unable to leave her bed. And, unable to stay away, he headed in to see her.

She was once again attempting to get out of bed. With a wince and gasp of pain she relented and sat back on the mattress where Mrs. Garrison set the tray. Harlow seemed almost angry with the limb that refused to support her weight as if it had failed her in some way.

He didn't know the woman well, but already he'd gathered she wasn't one for sitting still for very long. He was much the same way. And he disliked not having anyone to talk with. Which was the reason he had arrived so early in the day. He liked that they had that in common. But then not many people would like being forced to lie about.

Once she was settled again and staring longingly at the window, he knocked and entered her room.

"How are you feeling today, Lady Harlow?"

"Better, thank you. Though I do wish I could get out of bed."

He smiled with the pleasure of having guessed correctly, though it was a silly thing.

He hoped he would be correct in the reason for his visit that morning. She may not be able to get around very well with her injury, but he knew how they might pass the time.

"*The Case of the Rook's Tower?*" She said as he held up the book as he stepped closer. "I've not heard of it."

"That's because it only comes out next month. I have an early copy from the author herself."

He chuckled again when Harlow narrowed her eyes in disbelief. My, but her brothers must have deviled her something fierce to have caused such an inherent doubt about everything. He wished he could have been there to protect her from them. Ironically, they would likely wish to be here to protect her from him as well.

"Shall I read it to you?" he offered.

"We should take turns," she countered. "It's only fair."

"Very well, let us begin."

They spent the rest of the day reading to each other. As he listened to her, he found the low, almost raspy quality of her voice alluring in a way he shouldn't feel about an injured maiden in his care. He piled that onto the growing list of infractions he was guilty of since she'd arrived.

She was lovely despite her long, dark hair hanging in a simple braid over her shoulder, and the much-too-large dressing gown engulfing her luscious form. She was not so thin as the debutantes he'd encountered in the ballrooms this year.

She was muscled from physical activities the ton likely wouldn't approve of. But he preferred it. It was clear to him she did not spend all her time indoors reading Stonecliff novels.

Twenty-six proposals in her first season.

It was no wonder. Had he been looking for a wife, he might have been in line as well. And then it would have been twenty-seven refusals.

Thinking of rejected proposals stung the small wound still healing from Miss Sheridan. While he knew the two of them would not have made a happy match, he couldn't help but consider how the only women eager to marry him were those whose families were desperate for funds.

None of them truly *liked* him. Or had even spent more than a few moments to get to know him. Was that all he offered of value? Money?

No. He knew well enough it wasn't just the money. His title was in high demand as well. The rank of countess attracted the wealthy but lower ranking merchants' daughters.

He blamed Finn and Shay for his sudden desire to find more than just a marriage. He now wanted a happy match as they had. And if he was not expecting love as his friends found, he wanted friendship and respect. And if not those, at least someone willing to sit and read with him.

He looked at the woman whose eyes were growing heavy as she read and thought he understood why she had not accepted anyone's proposal. She was hunted for the same reasons. Not for herself, but for the money her dowry afforded or the thrill of securing a duke's daughter.

They were alike in that way. Both avoiding interest, while feeling as if no one really wanted them.

When her words drifted off, he again watched her sleeping for longer than he'd ever admit. He stood and slipped the book from her hands to set it on the stand next to the bed. Then picked up the candle and left the room, leaving her in darkness so she might have a restful sleep.

In his own room, however, sleep did not come so easily. There were many things to think about.

If he were to go to Inverness, he might have the chance to face the man that nearly killed him. The scoundrel who had forced Reese to relive the horror in his dreams was only a day's ride away. Up until he'd been shot, Reese had lived in the foolish disbelief he was invincible; he was now well aware of the blinding truth that it wasn't so.

That everything could end in a fleeting moment. Of course, he'd known of young men who'd met their ill-timed fate early in life, though he'd lost no one close to him in that way. For the most part, Reese always assumed death came for those who had roamed the earth for their set amount of time and then faded off into the peaceful bliss of the unknown.

But now, Reese was shaken by the abruptness of how quickly it could all come to an end. Too soon. And he blamed Captain Merrick for it. The man was deadly and was a burden to the Crown, but it wasn't solely Reese's loyalty to the Crown that had him seeking vengeance on this maritime menace.

He could have another chance to face the man and bring him to justice. He'd done the right thing to alert the authorities. They would take care of Merrick while Reese—now a civilian—was able to stay at Slains and take care of Harlow. No one would question why he didn't see to the duty himself. He was an earl and these messy affairs were left to agents, not noblemen.

Still, he wondered if it should be him that brought the man to justice. Would the night terrors relent if he personally saw the man swinging from the end of a rope? If he could see the matter dealt with, he'd have no reason to be continually haunted by the monster.

He might have gone if he wasn't needed at home to see to Harlow.

# Chapter Seven

HARLOW'S EYES OPENED to a bright room. As sleep cleared, she was reminded where she was and why. Belle raised her head from where she lay next to Harlow. The dog was a faithful guardian, never leaving her side for very long.

Though Harlow knew from the scent of wet fur and saltwater, that the dog often spent the early morning by the ocean. Today, however, she didn't.

As Harlow had done every day for the last week, she started the day by attempting to get out of bed and testing her weight on her injured ankle. Hoping this would be the day she was healed enough to get out of bed.

She was not certain how it had become so badly damaged from jumping into water, but Reese explained that it could have happened as she'd washed ashore. She recalled hurting her foot on the ship when she was hurrying toward the shadows. The flash of fire that was doused by fear and determination.

Harlow didn't remember much after she'd jumped over the rails of the Zephyr. Just the shocking chill of the water and the darkness. She'd managed to find the oar she'd thrown overboard, and the small chunks of wood on the net had floated as well. She'd kicked her feet pointing herself toward what looked like mountains in the distance. Land.

But it was too far and her head hurt to the point of dizziness. She remembered the panic she'd felt when her body failed her. Her legs were like leaden weights pulling her under, unable to kick anymore, while her mind seemed ready to accept defeat. She'd had no fight left.

*Death would not be so bad.* She recalled that final thought before she'd simply given up and rested her head on the smooth wood of the bobbing oar.

Realizing what might have happened kept her from complaining over her ankle now. It could have been so much worse.

*Perspective*, she thought the word yet again. She'd never really had reason for her perspective to shift so greatly before. But here she was in a strange man's home, unchaperoned and grateful for only having an injured ankle after her ordeal.

She pulled the ill-fitting dressing gown tighter around her when there was a knock at the door.

"Is it any better today?" Reese asked as he entered the room, groomed and dressed for the day.

"It's better each day, but still not fit for walking about," she said, doing her best not to sound irritable.

"I have a surprise for you," he said with a smile.

"A surprise?" She did love surprises, though she couldn't know what he might have for her.

He opened the door and stepped aside as a number of footmen came in carrying a tub and buckets of hot water.

A bath sounded divine, but it was what Mrs. Garrison carried in her arms that made Harlow's lips turn up in a smile.

"Is that a gown?"

"Aye," Reese said. "And a new shift and some other things you needed. I ordered them a few days ago and picked them up this morning. I shall leave you ladies to things and when you're dressed, I'll see you down to the dining room for breakfast."

She might have questioned how exactly she would get downstairs for breakfast, but the man simply gave a nod before he followed the footmen from the room, leaving her alone with the older woman.

"It's good to see you up, even if you can't get around so well yet. Here, lean on me and I'll help you over to the bath."

"I try not to complain about the inconvenience. Things could have been much worse if the earl hadn't found me when he did." She wanted to feel as grateful as she sounded.

"'Twas Belle who found ye."

Harlow smiled. "I shall give her extra petting for her heroism."

"She already thinks the world of ye." The woman nodded toward the dog who had rarely left Harlow's side since she'd arrived at Slains Castle.

"She is a good guardian. She's always there when I wake up."

"Aye. The earl is often watching over you as well."

"When I'm sleeping, you mean?" she asked the woman who just blinked at her for a moment before answering.

"I would never speak of it."

Harlow would have liked to point out that the housekeeper had indeed spoken of it already, but it was at that moment that Harlow's body slipped into the warm, fragrant water with a groan of happiness. Mrs. Garrison helped her wash her hair and then let her sit for a bit before coming back with linens to dry her off.

It wasn't an easy thing, getting out of the tub, but they managed. And then the woman saw to dressing her, drying her hair, and putting it up.

"I imagine you feel more like yourself, though it's been many years since I've done a lady's hair. I'm afraid I don't have the skills of your lady's maid."

"It is lovely. Thank you, Mrs. Garrison." It was enough that her hair was clean and had been brushed and put up out of the way. After all these days of sitting around, just being upright was a blessing.

But she looked toward the door, assuming she was upstairs while the dining room was likely on the floor below. How was she to get down there? She looked to the housekeeper who was heading for the door.

"Yer welcome, my dear. Now excuse me, I must see to the morning meal," she said before leaving the room.

Harlow sat in a nearby chair and was contemplating her next move when two swift knocks on the door were followed by its opening by a smiling earl.

"I hear you are ready to come downstairs."

"Yes," she answered, thinking he was going to offer his arm and the two of them would make their way to the breakfast room, hopefully before luncheon.

But instead he bent and lifted her into his arms.

"Put me down," she said in some surprise. It was completely improper being held against his strong body as she was. Not that every minute since she'd arrived hadn't also been improper, but this was beyond necessity.

"I certainly will," he said, but instead of doing so he moved through the open door and down the hall. He continued down the stairs and into the room, setting her back on her feet—or rather foot—next to the chair directly to the right of the head of the table.

Belle had followed along but was detoured at the door by one of the footmen.

"There you are. I put you down. Just as ye asked," Reese said, seeming pleased with himself.

Harlow might have contested his methods, but decided the smells of bacon and toast were more important at the moment. She slid into her seat allowing him to push her closer to the table.

Taking the seat next to her, he picked up his napkin and gave it a snap before settling it over his lap. She did the same only with less exuberance and they were served immediately.

"I thought after we eat you may enjoy a stroll through the garden. It's a lovely day. Belle could use the exercise, and I daresay you could use some sun now that your megrim has finally relented."

She agreed easily, focusing on the food. It had only been the last three days that her head had stopped making her nauseous. Her appetite had returned a little more each day, and this morning she was rather ravenous.

She managed to use her cutlery and take small ladylike bites as was proper, but only just so, for she was so famished she wanted to pick up the rasher with her hands and strip it bare, with her teeth.

It was only when her stomach was full that she recalled his plans for the day. A stroll through the garden? Did he think she was going to allow him to carry her through the entire garden?

"I'm sorry, my lord, but I believe a stroll through the garden is beyond me as of yet."

"Not true."

She shook her head. "I'll not be carried all that way."

"Nay, and I'd not make it to carry you all that way."

She frowned, knowing there was an insult there, but not willing to pick at it. She was in no way dainty like the young misses in the ballrooms. She preferred to go riding and walking daily. She preferred to be in motion when possible. And she enjoyed cake immensely.

"I might manage with a cane," she reasoned.

"I've sent for something better." He nodded to one of the footmen who left the room only to return seconds later pushing a wheeled chair.

"Oh," Harlow managed with a smile. "Where…?"

"I knew my good friend, Granton, had one for his dear sister who passed. I sent a gig to pick it up. It only arrived last evening."

He assisted her into the chair and wheeled her out onto the terrace. From there he maneuvered a few stone steps to get them down to the path.

For a while the only sound was of the waves crashing and the wheels rolling over the crushed shell walkway. Though she couldn't see the ocean, she could hear it. She was about to ask when Belle ran ahead chasing after something she spotted in the brush.

Harlow leaned her head back to allow the sun to warm her face. It was a lovely day.

The soft chuckle behind her distracted her.

"What is funny, my lord? Have you never seen a person enjoy being outside before?"

"I've only known women to hide away from the sun for fear of getting spots."

Harlow smiled.

"If my mother was here, she would well remind me. But I believe it is too late anyway." She pointed to her nose. "I already have them. All the years running with my brothers in the summer."

He made a show of squinting at her face as if he couldn't see the freckles across her nose.

"I don't know why they're not more accepted. I think them lovely. Proof of a life lived outside, enjoying the world around us."

"Perhaps you can sway all of Society to think like you so I will be the height of fashion next Season."

"Next Season when you search for a husband?" he mentioned.

She wished she could see his face, but his being behind her as he pushed the chair made it impossible to know his expression.

"Searching makes it sound almost diabolical. I surely would never trap anyone or even wish to persuade them into considering me. I just want to be open to the idea so I will not face the rest of my life alone. I feel as if I was given a second chance. I don't wish to waste it."

Her chair paused in its motion for a moment. She felt Reese stand upright rather than where he'd been hunched to reach the chair. What had she said that had surprised such a reaction from him?

"And of course, I will need to find another man who is not put off by freckles. Do you think there may be more of you, Lord

Breckenridge?"

She shifted to the side so she might look over her shoulder at him. He was smiling.

"I think you'll find many a man is not so put off by them. Especially not when the nose they are on belongs to a lovely woman."

Was he flirting with her?

She supposed she should use the opportunity to sharpen her skills of flirtation as well, but for the life of her she couldn't think of anything to say.

"Promise me you will not accept the first buck who proposes," he said.

She'd told him she planned to do just that, but now days later she saw how rash that might be. Still she wanted to marry.

She frowned. "I'll not accept an offer only to accept. But if the first buck who proposes meets my criteria, then I don't care much for the order in which I'm asked."

"And what is your criteria?" he asked as she assumed he would. She also knew if she said she wasn't willing to discuss it, he would let it lie. As any well-mannered gentleman would. But she wanted to tell him. If only so she might know if her demands were too unreasonable.

"First, he must have a sense of humor. Not just fake charm as to laugh at my jests, but he must be able to make me laugh as well. I don't wish to spend my life unamused."

"Ah, should he wear a tasseled hat like a court jester?"

She shook her head. "There is a difference between being silly and being witty, and you well know it, my lord."

"You think I know the difference because I, myself, am witty? Gracious. Have I unwittingly met one of your criterium?"

She laughed as he'd, no doubt, intended. She found flirting to be easier than she'd expected. Perhaps that was because of her partner.

"Breathe easy, my lord. It is but one of the criteria, you are in no danger."

"Very well, then let's hear the rest of the list."

She swallowed for fear that telling him the rest of the list would not put his mind at ease. But there was one thing on her list she knew would disbar him from the competition.

"I would like a man who is kind," she said.

"If you'll recall, I did carry you to the safety of my home and care for you. I would say that's not just kind, but gallant as well. Is being gallant on the list?"

"Gallant is not on the list." Though she silently added it for it was a nice attribute indeed. "I would point out that you didn't care for me yourself, but had others do it for you."

He made a disgruntled sound behind her.

"I've read to ye. I carried you down to breakfast this very morning and secured a chair so ye might take the air. That took some care, I think."

"All right. You are kind. Two things on the list."

"And gallant would be a third," he mumbled just loud enough for her to hear. She wouldn't admit she'd added it.

"Patience," she blurted out because it was important and he obviously had none.

"Hmm…" He pondered for a few seconds. "I have my moments of patience, but would not say I am a very patient person in general."

"I have little to no patience, therefore the man I marry will need to have enough for both of us."

"Like charm and humor, I would debate that patience should nay be confused with level-headedness. For I'm quite level-headed and I believe, given the way you were able to calmly escape the clutches of a ship full of marauders, you are very level-headed as well."

"It may be true that patience could be exchanged evenly with level-headedness as I'm not sure what benefit true patience gets one."

"Unless ye plan to sit in silence for great lengths of time, or you become tedious, I agree. I don't see that patience would be such a desirable trait."

"I'm not willing to remove it from my list, but will take your points under advisement."

He parked the chair next to a bench and took a seat. She looked around noticing the bird flitting about. But before she had the chance to grow weary of the silence, he spoke again.

"What else is on the list?" he asked as if the silence was bothering him as well.

"He must enjoy living in the country, for I prefer it."

"You do?" He tilted his head as if surprised.

"Yes. While our country home in Lancashire is not as vast as your castle in Scotland, it provides peace and quiet the city doesn't afford."

He laughed.

"What is wrong with wanting peace and quiet?" she pushed.

"Nothing at all, but I'm having trouble aligning the words *peace and quiet* with the picture you painted of you and your brothers. It sounded like a great deal of chaos and noise."

He had her there, still she refused to let him know.

"All the more reason I crave it now." That wasn't exactly true. She rather disliked quiet. Her mind seemed to fill the silence with thoughts of things she should have done or not done.

"It's never quiet here," he said. "Not with the sea constantly flinging itself against the cliffs creating a constant hum."

"I've noticed. But I don't see the ocean."

"It is that way," he pointed. "And then down many flights of stairs to get to the shore. We won't be descending them today."

She nodded. "I find the vibrations through the stone calming."

"I see," he said, not agreeing or disagreeing with her. She waited but he said nothing else on the matter so she delivered the final and perhaps the most important item on the list.

"I want a father for my children."

"I believe any man ye choose would be happy to provide children."

Seeming unsettled, he stood and began pushing the chair again. It was yet again one of those improper things. They surely shouldn't speak of children and definitely not how a man might want to get his wife with child.

She might have let it go, but she shook her head.

"No. I don't just want a man to sire children. I want a man who will be a real father. Like my own father. The duke did not leave us in our nursery, only calling upon the heir when needed. But he loves all of us. Many times he would be out in the fields playing next to us. I want that love for my children as well."

"So it is revealed. Your list was somewhat sensible, but now you speak of a love match."

She let out an annoyed sigh and tried to twist to look at him, but he was looking away. She let out a sigh.

"Of course, the first mention of emotions and the man begins to cast stones. I am not a silly girl, my lord. I understand finding a match is difficult enough and that demanding love be involved is a fantasy. Requiring love would diminish my chances to nothing, I would think. No, I do not require love between me and my husband, but friendship and respect. What I hope is that he would love his children, for it seems the simplest thing to do."

Reese had stopped pushing the chair and after a long silence he cleared his throat. "I don't think you have noticed the flowers over here at all. I'll take you closer."

She didn't know what she had said that had rattled the earl, but it was clear enough she had. Perhaps the man realized he had more attributes on her list than first thought.

Not that it mattered, for his proposal had been wrought by duty and honor rather than any real desire to take her as his wife. Lord Breckenridge might meet all the criteria she'd wished for, but there was another she'd not mentioned for it was most important.

The man she married would want to do so, and it was clear Reese did not.

# Chapter Eight

BY GOD, THE woman vexed him. At times like these when her thoughts aligned so closely to his own he wondered if she was a siren caught up on the land. But rather than lure him to the depths, she tempted him to do very ungentlemanly things. Like kiss her.

But kissing would surely lead to marriage and while he held most of the criteria on her list, he had already asked only to be refused. Or tried to ask. She'd cut him to the quick before he'd even had the words out. He wouldn't ask a second time only to be rejected yet again.

What she'd said about wanting a man who would be a loving father to her children had touched him in a tender place he'd thought had healed over years ago after his own father's death.

His father was all the things a typical father should be. He'd taught Reese to ride, hunt, and fence. He'd explained how the earldom should be run and the way to earn the respect of his people. He'd seen Reese educated so he could maintain the books properly, and even provided advice on what to look for when it was time for him to choose a wife.

However, Reese couldn't say whether or not the man loved him. One might say all of that was proof of love. But the auld earl had never hugged him or spoke of being proud of him. Had he been mean or cruel it might have been easier for Reese to have protected himself. The distance between them felt so close as though Reese might reach his father if only he tried just a bit harder.

And try he had to no avail. Perhaps it was his first rejection and why he wasn't willing to put himself in that position ever again.

Reese considered what being a father would mean to him as he finished the walk with Harlow and went to his rooms to change for dinner that evening.

He'd seen the way Finn had taken to the role of being a father with William. There would be no doubt in the boy's heart that his father loved him. Reese wanted to be the same kind of man with his children. So they might never wonder if they were good enough.

"You've been quiet since our walk. Did I say something to upset you, my lord?" Harlow asked as the meal was taken away and they were alone once more.

"No," he said, before telling her the truth. "It is what you said about how a father should be able to love his children. I'm not sure my father loved me."

"Was he cruel?" The way her face scrunched up amused him as if she would take up for Reese against his dead father. Of course, he shouldn't have been surprised. She was a woman set on vengeance. Apparently, it need not be her own.

"Nay. He was present and kind. But there was a wall between us I was unable to penetrate."

"But you tried."

"I dinna realize how very hard I'd tried until I considered it today."

"I'm sorry I upset you."

He shook his head. "I think I feel better actually. I've thought on it most of the day and I wonder if he was afraid of loving me. You see I had an older brother who died before I was born. I wonder if he'd loved Richard and after he lost him his heart was too broken to love me. Maybe he feared the pain he'd endure if something happened to me as well."

Harlow stood and hobbled the few steps to put her hand on his shoulder.

"I'm sorry, Reese." Hearing his name on her lips stirred something in him, but he cleared his throat and after giving her hand a squeeze in silent gratitude, he pointed to her chair.

"Ye should not be on that ankle. Do you want it to heal or no?"

She fell back into her seat and allowed him to lighten the mood once again.

Later that evening as he lay in bed, he cast off the thoughts of his father and recalled the list of criteria Harlow had wanted in a husband.

She'd joked that he was safe from being a viable candidate, but he realized now that he wanted many of the same things in a wife as she did in a husband. It would seem they were more matched than was comfortable.

He could not allow himself to want Harlow Haverston, for if he proposed and she rejected him again, he might never get over it.

⟫⟫⟫❮❮❮❮

TWO MORNINGS LATER, Harlow got out of bed to try her ankle and it held firm. She gasped with joy this time instead of pain.

"Look at this," she said to the dog who had lifted her large head only to settle it back on the covers. "Well, I am quite happy."

Harlow rang for Mrs. Garrison who came in and smiled to see her walking around.

"Oh, how wonderful! It's healed." Mrs. Garrison gave the proper effort of excitement.

"Yes. It feels wonderful to be able to move where I want."

"Just don't overwork it too soon or you'll be back to the wheeled chair."

Harlow nodded with a smile on her lips. Her mother had told her often how the little things matter most. The duke had enough money to buy the duchess nearly anything she could want, but it was acts of kindness that touched her mother's heart.

Harlow thought she might understand it more now that she'd had an attractive man do something sweet for her.

"It was very kind of him to send for it," Harlow said out loud.

"The earl is a kind man. He'd do the same for anyone," Mrs. Garrison said and Harlow frowned slightly. Of course, he was only being kind as he would for any guest, or rather damsel, who landed on his shore in distress.

"Of course," Harlow agreed.

A few moments after Harlow had been dressed and her hair was fixed, there was a knock at the door which she opened herself.

Lord Breckenridge looked her over as she stood there on her own.

"It doesn't hurt ye?" he confirmed.

"No. It's healed. I'll be ready to walk next to you in the gardens today."

Belle pushed past them to take the stairs while Reese stayed by her side offering his arm as she took the steps slowly. It wouldn't do to turn her newly-healed ankle on the stairs and be back to relying on everyone to move her about. Besides, linking her arm with the earl's was no hardship.

He seemed to relax when she was seated in the chair next to his.

"In a few more days you might be able to make the stairs down to the shore," he said. "But not yet. The steps are quite steep and are often damp with mist."

She knew Reese went on daily walks along the shore with Belle. The dog would return with a wet coat smelling of dog and the sea, while the earl just smelled of salty air.

"I look forward to accompanying you," she said, meaning it more than she probably should. Without the haze of her brother's warnings, she could see the man before her more clearly. He was no longer a man not acceptable for marriage, but a kind man she was beginning to like too much.

For he'd already attempted to propose and it wasn't likely he'd offer again. And she didn't want him to suggest such a thing as a solution to the problem of her possible ruination.

She wanted him to want her. That is she wanted the man who would be her husband to choose her. Not Reese specifically, of course.

When breakfast was cleared away he asked if she was up for a short walk in the garden and she was a bit overenthusiastic in her reply.

"I can think of nothing I would want more."

"Nothing, eh?" He tilted his head toward the sky. "You prefer walking in the gardens to finding out what happens at the end of *The Rook's Tower?*"

"Yes. At least for now. I love to be outside." Belle came back with a stick and nudged Reese with it. He took it and gave it a good toss as if he had done it a million times. When Belle returned it only a moment later, Harlow thought she might be right. "Being stuck inside for so long makes me want to enjoy it even more. It seems Belle feels the same way."

He shook his head. "Don't let her fool ye. She's been out for a walk every morning usually when ye were still asleep. But I know what you mean. I had an injury close to a year ago and was stuck in my bed for even longer than you had been. Once I was able to get up and move around I didn't wish to be back in my bedchamber. In fact, I slept in my study for a few nights."

She nodded in understanding. "What happened?"

"Oh," he waved it off as if it were nothing. "Just a bit of trouble with my leg. It's fine now."

She sensed he didn't wish to speak of it, so she changed the subject.

"It is beautiful here." It was true enough, but the man next to her was the best part. Though one could argue the man and the lands were alike in many ways. Both had a... contained wildness about them.

The way the manicured gardens flirted at the edges of the unkempt tree line made her think of the well-mannered man beside her who edged the lines of propriety. The cultivated and the rough parts. Even his speech toyed along the borders. Speaking with an educated tongue weighed with the brogue of his home.

"I enjoy being here," he said.

"You can be yourself," she guessed, though should have probably kept it to herself. She had grown too comfortable with him. It was likely the reason for her earlier thoughts of marriage and children with the earl.

When he smiled she felt a tingle in her stomach.

"Yes. I'm sure it is similar in the way you shed all the rules of London when you are in Lancashire?"

She nodded. "Yes. I might shed more rules than I ought."

"Oh? You've piqued my curiosity. What do you do in the country that would make the ladies of the ton gasp in dismay?"

"Surely, I'll not tell you."

"After I opened my home to ye and let you claim my dog."

"You cannot blame me if she likes me better." She offered a saucy shrug which caused him to huff a laugh.

"I dare you?" His lips pulled up in a crooked grin.

Oh, the beast. He didn't have siblings, but he must have spent time with other children in school. He'd likely guessed the way her brothers dared her to do things and she'd been unable to turn away from any challenge.

"Very well. I wear men's breeches when I ride in the country."

"Eh. That's not so scandalous. I would guess many women do the same."

"Not scandalous?" she said in shock. But he'd acted as if it was nothing of note. If he was not surprised by that she would tell him something sure to win this contest. "I swim at night. Naked."

She knew she was the victor when his eyes flared with warm heat. He turned toward her, his dark brown eyes flicking side to side as he clearly studied her face. As if looking for proof of a lie. Did he think she'd made up such a claim?

If so, he could look all he wanted and never see her waver, for it was the truth.

"Only when it's very warm, and I'm sure my brothers are away or in their beds. Only when I know I'm completely alone do I remove my wrapper and night rail and slip into the chilly water as the moon and stars provide the only light."

He swallowed. She saw him do it. Just as she saw him bend his head as if he planned to kiss her. Her heart hammered in her chest as she quickly decided whether to stop him or grab him close so he would do it faster.

But then they both jumped when Mrs. Garrison shouted for him. It was then as she turned toward the housekeeper that she heard another noise. Carriage wheels on crushed shells.

Someone was here.

---∙———∙◆∙———∙———

# Chapter Nine

G OOD GOD, REESE had been seconds from kissing the woman. No, not simply kissing her, but claiming her. For he was short on control as she spoke of her nights spent bathing in moonlight and nothing more.

He imagined the way she would pin the mass of her hair up so it wouldn't get wet, only to have the weight of it fall down her back to curl in the water. He envisioned the way her nipples would tighten as she descended into the cool, dark lake. And then the way the moisture would make trails down her skin as she stood. Each droplet merging with another as they traced their way along each glorious curve.

He'd grown hard just thinking of it. He was grateful she was studying his face or she would have clearly seen the way his breeches failed him and modesty.

Since they'd spoken yesterday of the things she wanted in a mate, Reese had been making his own mental list of his criteria. Willing to swim naked during the summer evenings was now at the top of his list.

He'd already been amused to think of her riding in men's breeches. He'd done his best to downplay his interest in such a thing. For imagining her arse being caressed in a saddle in tight-fitting fabric had stirred him.

He'd made a grave error to taunt her. She had clearly won.

"If you'll excuse me," he said abruptly and turned for the house, leaving her there in the garden. She'd been pleased that her ankle would hold her, which meant she could find her way back to the house without his assistance. It was still rude for him not to provide escort back to the house, but ruder still would be for her to catch a glimpse of how she had affected him.

Stealing into the entrance of his study from the terrace, he pressed against his aching cock as if that would make it go away. Closing his eyes tightly he conjured a memory of when he was a boy and was forced to eat haggis. It hadn't gone well for him. The memory was just horrible enough to cool his blood.

When he'd reigned himself into control, he exited the study for the front of the house to greet his guest.

"Albert?" Reese said having recognized the man who was handing Finch his hat and coat.

"Reese! How do you fare? How's the leg?" the man asked. He knew about Reese's run-in with Merrick. Not only because he was an agent himself, but because he was there that night on the docks when Reese had been shot. He'd been the one who had found him and taken him to the surgeon, saving Reese's life.

He owed the man more than a hearty greeting, but that's what he could offer at the moment. At least until he'd learned why the man had come.

"What brings you this far north?"

"Your letter to the home office. I was sent to intercept the Zephyr in Inverness. That's where it's moored, yes?"

"Aye. That's where it was headed eight days ago. I'd imagine it is still there." The man must have ridden as if the devil was chasing him to get here so quickly, but it was nothing Reese wouldn't have done himself back in his days as an agent. "It would not be a quick thing to offload smuggled brandy and whatever other contraband fills its holds. Please tell me there is more than just you on this mission."

Albert chuckled.

"Yes. Evershire and Willard have ridden on ahead to gather men in Inverness. Hopefully, we're not too late. The man is like the mist."

"Merrick will also be waiting there to receive a ransom for the lady. He will not be leaving until it arrives."

"Even though he no longer has her?"

"I'm sure he'd think her dead after she jumped overboard."

Albert nodded his agreement. "She's a brave one. Many a miss would have cowered in a corner. I'd like to interview her. Learn how she escaped."

"We can ask, but if she is uncomfortable discussing it, I'll not allow her to be upset."

"Of course," Albert agreed. But Reese saw the flare of curiosity in the man's eyes. He'd held the same desire for knowledge when he'd been the one asking the important questions. It was an easy thing to forget how fragile a person could be during the retelling of something distressing. He'd been guilty of it many times in his search for information. He'd not allow Harlow to be pressured into sharing more than she wished.

"If she refuses, that is the end of it."

"Of course," Albert repeated and gave a nod as well.

"My mother is in residence as Lady Harlow's chaperone. You may not see her during your visit, but the lady's reputation will not be called into question, do you understand?" If the man didn't hear the threat in the tone of Reese's voice, he surely saw it in the cock of his brow.

"I believe I did see your mother in an upstairs window as I was coming down the drive," the agent said though Reese was certain the man had never even met his mother so even if she had been at Slains he'd not know it. Albert only wanted the information needed to capture Merrick; anything else was irrelevant. But there was one more thing Reese needed to address.

"And you'll not tell her of my being an agent."

"You aren't an agent anymore. Nothing to tell," Albert said surely with a nod.

With a nod of his own, Reese went to get Harlow.

AFTER THE EARL'S abrupt departure in the gardens, Harlow and Belle had finished their walk and were sitting on the terrace. She wasn't sure where Reese would take his guest to visit, and Harlow didn't want to be seen at Slains Castle with no chaperone.

It would be a miracle if she could make it home with her reputation intact, but she would do her best not to make any reckless mistakes that would otherwise seal their fate.

For if Harlow was publicly ruined, her father would demand Reese marry her. Something she couldn't bear. Neither of them wanted to be forced to wed. She'd not be the cause of such an outcome.

She was seated on a bench, rubbing Belle behind the ears the way the dog seemed to like best when the earl came out through his study.

He didn't speak until he sat next to her, taking up rubbing the dog's other ear.

"There is a man here. His name is Albert. He's an agent with the Home Office, sent here to look for Captain Merrick and take him into custody for crimes against the Crown."

"I see," she said, glad her voice didn't tremble. For she didn't see. She'd never been mixed up in such serious things before. The Home Office, agents, treasonous captains that kidnap innocent women… It was all the stuff of novels. But she was living it now. She focused on Reese's face as he continued.

"He would like to question you about the events that brought you here. I told him only that I would ask. No one will make you, do you understand?"

She nodded and opened her mouth to explain that she'd be more than pleased to help bring the captain to justice if not for the danger to her reputation, but Reese spoke as if he already knew what worried her.

"He's been sworn to secrecy regarding the nature of your visit here. I assured him my mother was in residence, and he has agreed. No one will know any differently, I promise ye. But it is still up to you if you wish to speak of what happened."

"I can do it. If it means having the man stopped. I want to help."

"I thought ye might. You're a brave lass." He looked out over the grounds before looking back at her. "I will stay with you while you tell him the story. But if you were to speak of your uncle's part in this, he would surely be arrested."

Harlow looked up at him to see what he thought of this, but he gave nothing away.

"If Uncle Edgar is arrested, he wouldn't be able to come here. I'd not get to see him again. Not get to hear him explain himself or see him beg for forgiveness he will never get."

"He would likely be dealt with along with Merrick. It is likely to be a severe punishment, Harlow. I want to make sure you understand what could happen."

She understood. But there was something else she had wondered and needed to know before she went any further.

"It may be some time yet until he arrives. When I first planned revenge, I didn't give much thought that you might not want me here so long. With my ankle recovered, I could return home."

He nodded slowly without looking at her.

"You are welcome to stay in my home for as long as you wish. I'd not cast ye out no matter the length of your stay and surely not after you've been back on your feet for less than a day."

She nodded. It was what she had expected any gentleman to offer. But he hadn't said he wished her to stay. Was that because he wanted it to be her decision or because he truly didn't care.

"I will tell ye," he said looking her in the eye. "There is something to be said for getting closure on this event. You had no control over how you ended up on that ship, but you can take that back now. My leg… well, the person who did it got away, and I think the matter bothers me more because I wasn't able to see it through. That's why I'll help ye with whatever you need."

This time when she nodded she was more resolute. If she were not so set on seeing her uncle again and making him explain why he'd let her be taken, she might have been content to allow the authorities to handle it. But she needed to know why he'd betrayed her in such a painful way. She needed to look him in the eye while he told her the truth.

"I wish to handle him myself. I need to have my chance."

He nodded. "If you can relay the facts without mention of Polk it would serve your plans better. Try to keep to the truth as much as possible."

After a deep breath she took the hand he held out to help her up. She slid her arm over his so he could lead her inside, where she would give a stranger every detail of the worst moments of her life.

She closed her eyes for a second and gathered her strength around her. She would do this so no one else would fall victim to that monster.

# Chapter Ten

"Mr. Albert, may I make known to you Lady Harlow Haverston," Reese conducted the introductions while Harlow took her seat in the chair across from the stranger. She twisted her fingers, hoping it would stop her hands from shaking but guessed the twisting told the man she was nervous anyway.

"Lord Breckenridge wrote to us of a kidnapping and said you'd managed to escape Captain Merrick's ship. I assure you we are doing everything in our power to see the man is brought to justice."

"Justice?" she said aloud without meaning to. It had been a word she'd not given much thought to before her kidnapping. Now it occupied her thoughts a great deal.

"A long drop with a short rope, my lady."

Harlow heard the breath suck through her lips and Reese scolded the man.

"My apologies. I'm not one to spend time with proper ladies. My speech is too bold."

Of course, she knew criminals were hung as punishment for their crimes. It had been the main ingredient in most of her brothers' gruesome ghost stories when they'd been children. Always ending with a man who was hung but walked among the living with the noose still tied around his neck, searching for his next victim.

"It is all right, Mr. Albert. It's often one thing to know something, and quite another to speak of it. I assure you, I'm not too delicate for such topics."

Reese pressed his lips together likely in an attempt to hide his smile. He must have known how she didn't like for anyone to think her weak. Ignoring him, she focused on the man across from her who looked much too young to be an agent of the Crown.

His hair was a rather mousy shade of brown and his cheeks were bare of any hint of a beard, and full and round like a boy. In contrast, this time in the afternoon, Reese had a glistening of blond hair along his jaw. She wondered if it would be rough against her palm, and shook her head to dispel such improper thoughts. Now was no time to think of such things.

Mr. Albert's blue eyes held a bit of mischief, adding to his boyish looks, and they were focused intently on her now.

"Yes, my lady. Of course." He seemed as worried as she was, though she supposed his worry was over making another misstep that would have Reese kicking him from his home. "Would you tell me what happened when you were taken?"

Harlow gave a quick nod and then looked at Reese as she collected her thoughts. He gave her an encouraging smile and then a wink. Strange how such a gesture could fortify her. While also making her knees tremble. It was good she was sitting.

"It was early morning. My uncle and I were riding together in Hyde Park. I don't often stay to the regular paths. I prefer to be alone, or as alone as one can be in London. There's a path I usually take that's in a more secluded section of the park and that's where I was heading. But before I got to the trail, a number of men stepped out of the brush. So many."

"Do you know how many?"

As Harlow recalled, it had felt like a dozen or more but she focused on the details of each one and was sure it was not as many as it first seemed.

"Nine." She considered again and then nodded. She was sure that was correct. "Two of the men grabbed onto Brook's harness to stop him. The man that pulled me down from my horse was tall, taller than Lord Breckenridge. His head was shaved except for a single lock that came out of the top of his head. He had markings on his face. A series of dots across his nose and cheeks. And some lines on his forehead." That man was the one whom she most remembered. Mostly because he haunted her dreams some nights. "Another wiry man stuffed a cloth in my mouth which cut off my screams."

"Where was your uncle?" Albert asked.

"I'm not sure. I was hit in the head with something hard and lost consciousness." That was a lie.

Harlow remembered hearing Uncle Edgar begging. *"Please, please don't hurt—"* Later she realized it was likely an act. He was already aware of her fate and wouldn't fear the men he worked with.

"Hmm…" Albert said with a worried look. "It's almost as if they knew where you would be that morning and were waiting for you. It wasn't a random kidnapping. I'd thought they were looking for someone of wealth, but it seems they wanted you specifically."

"Her father is among the richest of the ton," Reese said.

She knew it was common knowledge that the Ardmere dukedom was one of wealth. But she hadn't realized how familiar Reese was with this information. She thought of all the men at the balls who'd sought her out for no other reason but the size of her dowry. They didn't care for her, they didn't care about her at all.

"Yes," Mr. Albert continued. "They may have been watching you for some time, waiting for the moment to strike."

"Was a request for ransom received?" she asked.

The man shrugged. "I left London straightaway. Other agents will handle the matter of the ransom letter when it arrives. Since we know you're safe, there'll be no reason to pay it."

Harlow nodded, knowing they had told her father to with-hold payment in the letter she'd sent to her brother.

"When did you wake up?" the man asked.

"Shortly before dawn the next morning." From there she told Mr. Albert every detail of what had happened in her escape. Well except for the part where she lost her accounts all over Reese's boots. She didn't think that was a relevant detail anyway.

"I hope you don't mind my saying, you are a courageous woman, Lady Harlow. It is a great honor to know you."

"I only did what anyone would do in order to survive."

"You would be surprised. I've seen many a person simply freeze up, unable to think of anything to free themselves. You not only came up with a brave plan, but carried it out to perfection. I'd say none of our best agents could have done it better."

She felt her cheeks warm under the man's praise, but she nodded her thanks for his kind words. She didn't think the plan was so perfect when she'd had to jump overboard. And she surely hadn't felt brave when she'd simply given up when she couldn't swim any longer. But she had survived and that was the most important part.

"We are going to track him down. You'll not need to worry about him anymore. I promise you that. In addition to smuggling, the man has been selling secrets to the French. He's a traitor to the Crown and will be hunted to the ends of the Earth."

Harlow was glad the man would be dealt with. Perhaps once she knew he was no longer out there somewhere, she might be able to sleep without nightmares. She'd never seen the captain, but her mind conjured up the most hideous faces. Grotesque creatures always reaching for her out of the shadows.

"Ye are welcome to stay the night. Have a meal," Reese offered.

"I thank you, my lord, but I must keep moving toward Inverness."

Reese nodded and went to the door to summon Mrs. Garrison. "Please bring some provisions that Mr. Albert can take with him."

"Right away, m'lord."

As they waited, Harlow's curiosity got the best of her.

"How is my uncle?" she asked the agent.

The man smiled sympathetically. "He is well, my lady. He managed to escape the men. He said they tried to take him as well, but he pulled a knife and was able to get free. He deeply regrets not being able to save you."

Harlow forced her lips into a smile.

"I'm certain he tried his best," she said, while inside, the cold darkness of hate crept deeper into her soul. Edgar Polk would pay for his treachery.

HARLOW WAS QUIET as they ate supper together. Reese imagined she had a lot on her mind with the information they'd received from their guest. Reese had wanted it to be an enjoyable day since she was mobile once again, but the visit from Albert had cast a shadow.

"I'm sorry if the agent upset ye today. You did a fine job providing details to help in the search of the men who hurt you," he praised her with the truth.

Often a person was able to push the worst parts of life away. As if locking them inside their own chest. But when they were called on to retell the details, the chest is unlocked and the demons of their memories are released to cause pain all over again.

"It's normal to have memories you don't want to think about swirling about in your mind after you stirred them up today."

"It is like any other wound, I imagine. It began to heal over, but talking about it tears them open again to bleed and hurt."

"Aye. It is just so."

"There is one thing it did help me with."

"Oh?" he asked.

"I think I know how I want to deal with my uncle."

He started in surprise. Harlow had vowed to get her revenge on the man who'd betrayed her, but she hadn't as yet settled on the details. He assumed they would lure the man here so she could face him and tell him how disappointed she was with him.

Reese didn't know Edgar Polk, but if he was a hardened man, her words would be unlikely to touch him. Men focused on such things as money are often left with no soul.

As the meal was cleared, he asked her to tell him of her plans.

"You may think it is a bit dramatic, but I want the man shaking in fear for his life. I'm not so terrifying, but I can be, with your help."

They remained at the table as they went through the details. At first, he was skeptical of how it might work, but soon he had sent for paper and ink so they might make a list of things they would need to carry out her plot.

He had to admit it was creative.

"It seems having five older brothers has come to your aid with devising a diabolical plan."

She nodded with a smile that didn't linger.

"I hope you don't think me foolish," she said after a moment of silence. "Going through all of this just to get back at him for what he did to me. It might seem childish."

"Nay. Not at all. I can think of many a person I'd like to line up for the same fate as your uncle."

She shook her head. "Not with the theatrical plan, but for my desire for vengeance."

He shrugged. "You were wronged by someone you trusted. Your uncle took something important from ye, it is understandable you would want to take it back."

"But that is just it. I will never get it back. When I'm finished with this ruse, I'll still be left with nothing but memories of a man who wasn't who I thought he was. Even if it goes according to plan and Edgar is kneeling at my feet, sobbing in fear and begging for forgiveness, what comes after? When he is taken away to face his fate, I will be left to face my own. Will I still be bound up in all this hatred? Will I be able to forgive him, or will I be destined to go mad with an unquenchable thirst for vengeance?"

"I have not known you long, but I think if he truly asks for forgiveness, if he sincerely regrets what happened, it will soothe the pain in your heart enough that you can move on."

"And if he doesn't regret it?"

Reese tapped the paper in front of him with their plans drawn out.

"He will. After this, I don't see how he could not."

❧ ⟨❀⟩ ☙

# Chapter Eleven

THE NEXT DAY, supplies arrived and Reese and Harlow worked tirelessly at setting up everything needed for her stage of sorts. He was impressed by her thoroughness to every detail.

"It must be as lifelike as possible," she said, not for the first time as they'd been working.

Reese hadn't even realized how much time had passed until Mrs. Garrison brought in the noon meal. Despite the macabre outcome, they'd had a great deal of fun creating everything.

"You don't need to dig so very far," she ordered later that afternoon, when he complained about the physical labor with the spade. "Do you want me to do it?"

His eyes went wide. Leave it to Harlow to offer to take over.

"What experience do you have with digging holes in the dirt, Lady Harlow?" he teased.

"More than you would think. I once got in a great deal of trouble for digging a hole and covering it in sticks and leaves. I hid in the bushes for Hen to walk by and get his foot caught in it. I wasn't expecting Miss Perkins, our nurse, to find it instead. She was laid up for some time." Harlow winced while Reese did his best not to laugh and failed.

"My, but you must have been quite the hoyden when you

were a lass."

"Some would say I'm still a hoyden today. I know my dowry held most of my appeal, but I wonder if anyone would find me suitable without it."

Reese wanted to tell her he enjoyed her vivacity quite a lot. He'd danced and spoken with a number of young ladies during the Season who were taught to keep their light hidden away. Instead speaking only of the dullest of topics. Harlow was refreshing and fun. In fact, he could envision a happy life for the man who married her. Whoever he turned out to be.

He winced at the prickly feeling in his stomach that came over him all of a sudden and for no reason at all. Clearing his throat, he told her what he thought.

"Someone who wishes to spend his life having a great deal of fun will offer for you without a thought to the money. And I know a lot of men who do not wish to give up on enjoyment when they marry."

"And these great lot of men… Are they already married?"

He winced. "Aye. Most of them."

Later as they had turned to the task of painting, Reese found himself watching as she concentrated on her letters. Did she know her tongue peeked out of her lips the tiniest bit when she focused so intently? He found it adorable, as he found too many things about her.

He imagined what it might be like if he was the man who got to spend his life with her and how he would never fear spending a moment in boredom. But she had rejected him already, so she was not to be his future. He would enjoy this time with her and think fondly of her when she left.

"Belle!" Harlow yelled when the dog came too close as to get black paint in her wiry coat. "I'm sorry."

"No need to apologize, it was her own fault and I can assure you, it's not the worst thing I've had to wash out of her fur."

As if trying to make amends, his dog came close and rubbed her head on his leg, essentially covering him in black paint.

"Thanks, old girl." He shook his head at the dog as Harlow giggled.

After their meal they spent the evening in the library reading to each other.

She had kicked off her half boots and had her small feet tucked up on the settee next to her. As she read, he became fixated on her toes as they wiggled inside her stockings and he imagined going over there and removing them so he might press a kiss to the arch of her foot before moving up to her dainty ankle. Then her calves and her knees. He would touch the inside of her thighs with the tip of his tongue and trace a line up to her—

"Reese?" she interrupted his thoughts, and it was clear by the crease between her brows it wasn't the first time she'd said his name. "Are you bothered by my feet on your furniture? I'd not think you so fussy when Belle is sprawled out on the other settee. My feet are surely cleaner than the dog."

"Nay. It doesn't bother me. I was just thinking of something else. The dress you will need for the scene in the garden."

"Ah. I will start working on it tomorrow. But now, it is your turn to read the next chapter. Unless you've grown tired."

"I'll read one last chapter and then we can go to our beds."

She hopped up and brought the book over to him. Their fingers touched as they passed it between them, and he felt the shock of it down to the place where he still throbbed. He was grateful she was able to bring the book to him as he would have been unable to stand to retrieve it himself.

As he settled into reading the story—feeling a bit lost as he had missed her reading most of the last chapter—he saw how his life could be with the right woman. He'd spent nearly every moment of the day with Harlow, yet he wished he didn't have to say goodnight. He could have happily spent the rest of the night with her. Especially doing the things he'd been considering earlier.

"Did you fall asleep?" she asked when he stopped speaking.

"Nay. I'm still awake. Sorry." He continued reading until the end of the chapter. When she didn't say anything, he looked over to find her sleeping. He took a moment to study her features. The way her perfect bow lips parted slightly. The way her dark lashes caressed her cheeks. That raven hair pulled back in a braid. Though like her, the locks had fought their way free throughout the day.

His gaze continued down her body, taking in each hill and valley to end with those small feet, just peeking out from under the edge of her skirt.

With a sigh, he stood and went to her. He should wake her. It was one thing to use her slumber to stare at her, but yet another to use it as a way to pick her up so he could hold her body against his. He reasoned that she would be too tired to climb the stairs to her room, and this would be the most expedient way to get her where she needed to be. But as soon as he settled her against him, he was cursed with the truth.

He wanted her. Physically, of course, for she was a beautiful woman, but that was not the extent of his desire. He wanted her smiles and laughter. He wanted her thoughts and stories. He wanted *her*.

"Bloody hell." He settled her on the bed and as Belle took her post at the woman's side, he left. In the hall, he'd hoped to regain control over his feelings but it seemed they would not relent.

He spent the first hours trying to sleep and failing. He was restless with thoughts of Harlow. Not just the surprise of how much fun he had had with her, but hearing her tell her story about her time on the Zephyr had called up memories of his moments with the vicious Merrick.

Thinking of what might have happened to her if she'd not escaped made him shift restlessly. To think he'd never have known her.

Soon he was back in that alley along the wharf where a French spy was expected to arrive soon enough. They would intercept the man—or woman—who arrived for the meeting and bring them in for questioning.

They hadn't expected Merrick to show up. He'd been a person of interest in a smuggling case as were many captains of sailing vessels at the time. But they hadn't realized until that night that he dealt in more than just silks and wine. He sold secrets.

When they had the spy apprehended, Reese had turned his attention on Merrick, running after him with a few other agents following. But Reese was closest. He'd not expected the man to suddenly stop running. Not until he'd seen the glint of the metal when the pistol was raised in Reese's direction.

He remembered seeing the flash in the dark night when the gun was fired. In the bright light he saw the smoke from the charge. And then he felt the thud as if he'd been hit by a herd of elephants as he fell to the damp wood of the dock.

Heat burned through him as he reached down for his leg, expecting to put out a fire. But there was no flame. His hand was instantly coated in thick, warm blood.

His vision began to falter as he looked to where Merrick had been. To his surprise he found the man still standing there. Nay, he was closer now. With a smoking weapon in one hand, he pulled the twin of that pistol from his coat and aimed it at Reese.

Past the opening of the barrel, Reese saw the man close one eye with an evil smirk on his lips. And then the loud bang of the second shot.

Reese knew then he was having a nightmare, for that night Merrick had not fired a second shot. The shouts of the other men coming closer had forced him to tuck the unfired weapon back in his coat as he ran off.

But it had been a close thing, and Reese knew that second shot would have been fatal.

He gasped for air as he woke to the bright room. He was covered in sweat, his hair and bedclothes wet. Somehow despite having been asleep, he was more exhausted than he'd been before he'd laid down the night before.

He called for a bath and took his time washing and getting

ready for the day. As was often the case, it took some time for him to be able to push away the fear left by the dream.

Things could have ended so differently for him that night. But he was alive and he'd at least been able to aid in Captain Merrick's capture. Albert would find the man in Inverness and capture him. And when the man was brought back to England to face his crimes, Reese would make sure to have a front row spot for his hanging.

And when the man's body had finished twitching, Reese hoped he'd finally be able to sleep soundly again.

HARLOW WOKE WITH a start. She'd been dreaming, as was common since her escape from the Zephyr, but instead of her imagination providing images of Merrick chasing her as hands grabbed at her, it was a different man and the hands touching her were not that of an enemy.

She'd dreamed of Reese. She'd recalled the scent of him, leather and the sea, as she'd slept. She'd noted it many times before, but yesterday they had worked closely together while painting and digging in the dirt. Sometimes their heads touching. It was easier to remember the way he'd smelled when her air had been filled with his scent.

She remembered the warmth of his hands as he'd taken the book from her, but also in all the times they'd touched for some reason or another. But in her dreams he'd touched her purposefully in places no man had ever touched her before.

She'd dreamed of him kissing her. And while she lacked the factual elements to make a true reproduction, the details her mind conjured up were quite pleasing. For whatever reason, she'd dreamed he'd tasted like Cook's lemon biscuits. Perhaps because they were her favorite.

She thought of the way he'd looked at her earlier that evening. She loved walking in the gardens with him and talking about the antics they got up to in their childhood. But the cozy evenings when they read to one another was peaceful in a different way than she'd ever known.

She was often busy, moving about to find something to occupy her restless energy, but when she was just lying on the settee listening to the low timbre, and soft brogue of Reese's voice, she felt calm. It was a place where she could happily belong.

She wondered if she'd been hasty when she'd rejected his proposal. She knew well enough he'd offered simply because he was a gentleman, playing her steadfast savior and nothing more. But still, perhaps if she'd accepted, they could have found happiness together. She certainly would have been happy with Reese.

She let out a breath and squeezed her eyes closed.

While the dream was pleasant for many reasons, it was not any less unsettling than her nightmares. For she was still left flustered, with her heart pounding. After a terror she would grab hold of good thoughts and hold on until daylight. But after this dream she wished it had not been morning so she might fall asleep again and pick up where she'd left off.

She doubted Reese would offer marriage again, as he didn't plan to marry. The way he'd sighed in utter relief when she'd stopped him, proved he was not truly interested in being her husband. But if he did have reason to offer again, she would be ready. And this time she might have a different answer.

# Chapter Twelve

Harlow looked tired when she came down to breakfast that morning, despite him knowing she'd been sleeping soundly when he'd left her in her room. Perhaps she'd woken uncomfortable for still being dressed. Mayhap he should have sent Mrs. Garrison in to help her change for bed.

He hadn't needed thoughts of Harlow in a night rail to add to his affliction. He'd taken matters in hand—quite literally—and was better equipped to face the day as they had previously. Before his urges had taken hold of him.

Harlow was a beautiful woman. She was funny and witty as well. But he need not lose his head. Or worse, his heart. For she didn't want him. Just as none of the other women he'd thought suited him had wanted him.

He empathized with Harlow for she searched for a man who would want her for herself, rather than her dowry. She was hunted for a bounty rather than for herself. He found himself in a similar predicament. Desperate women tried to trap him into marriage so they could be a countess, but they didn't care about him as a person. He was simply his title.

In a perfect world, he and Harlow would find each other and make an impeccable match. But it was not a perfect world. And he'd not lay himself open only to be rejected once again.

"You look tired this morning, my lord," Harlow said, stirring him from his silence.

"Odd. I was thinking the same of you. Did ye not sleep well?"

"I started out well enough, though I don't recall how I got to my bed." She raised a dark brow and he pointed at the dog sitting by the door.

"Belle grabbed you by your hair and dragged you up the stairs."

"Ah! That explains all the drool in my hair." She laughed and he joined her. He enjoyed how they teased each other in this way. Everything was so easy with her.

"I'm sorry. I should have sent in Mrs. Garrison to help ye dress more comfortably." He turned his gaze back to his plate so as not to have to see the pink flush on her cheeks. Oh, but she was even more lovely with color on her face.

"No matter. Belle assisted later when I woke. She bit through my laces to free me."

"Good lass," Reese said and flipped a piece of ham to the dog who eagerly accepted without a bit of guilt that she'd done nothing to deserve it.

Harlow laughed again and then when they had both resumed eating, she swallowed and said, "I had a dream."

"I'm sorry." He knew she'd been cursed with night terrors since her ordeal on the ship. Many a night as he'd sat by her bed watching over her, she had thrashed about, attempting to fight off the monsters of her dreams.

"It is not your fault. It's not as if they were of you," she said so quickly he thought she might be lying. When he was trained as an agent, he was taught to detect a lie. He'd even sought the help of his friend to test himself.

A lying person would seldom be able to look the other person directly in the eye, as Harlow was exhibiting now with her gaze drawn to the meat on her plate. They often fidgeted or attempted to deflect the conversation to some other topic, similar to the way she was hacking the ham to bits with her cutlery.

"I'd like to go down to the beach today," Harlow said as she tucked a non-existent lock of hair behind her ear.

He smiled as he watched her shift in her seat.

She had dreamed of him. She would never admit it, but he knew her well enough to know he was correct. What he wouldn't give to know the details of that dream. He'd consider giving up his very soul for the opportunity to make them reality.

"Your dreams must have frightened you terribly. People say talking about them helps," he kept his voice calm despite the way his heart was racing to push her to tell him.

"Oh, no. Thank you. That is, I don't need to speak of them. It's better they just…" She waved toward the stairs and her room beyond. "I know they aren't real."

"Hmm…" He frowned at his breakfast and let the subject drop.

They finished their meal in silence and the quiet continued as they descended the steep stairs to the beach. Even their footsteps made no sound where they walked in the sand. Belle had run off as was her way.

"She will return with something she's found on the shore. I shall pray it is only a stick."

Harlow chuckled. "Do you worry you may find another woman washed ashore?"

He looked up at the sky. "I guess I have plenty of room for a few more."

She smacked his arm lightly.

"I wish I could have seen your face when you found me."

"It was quite a shock. I'm guilty of hesitating for a moment or two before acting, for the thought did cross my mind it could be a trap to force me into marriage."

"I believe someone thinks himself quite the catch."

It was his turn to laugh.

"It would have been a diabolical plot, I agree. But once you live as I have, hunted by the fierce predators of the ton and their mamas, you become suspect of any possible entanglement."

"I don't know what the ladies were thinking."

"I believe they were thinking they wanted to be the Countess of Breckenridge. Nothing more."

"But what did they think would come of their life with you in the future? After they'd trapped you against your will, did they expect you to just smile and be happy with your lot so all was forgotten and forgiven?"

"I doubt there was much thought to the future. There was only the opportunity of that moment."

"What would have happened if they'd succeeded? If you were found in a compromising position and forced into marriage? What would you have done?"

It was a good question. One he'd not given much thought to since he'd managed to get free from the shackles of an unwanted match. He didn't like to think about it now.

For the first time he realized he might have been married to someone he didn't want when he found someone he did. What a travesty that would have been. He glanced at the woman walking next to him and did his best to cast the thought away.

"Well, I don't think I would have devised an elaborate ruse to get my revenge, if that's what you're asking."

"Revenge may have been extreme given the crime. That should be reserved for family members' cruel betrayals that risk the lives of others."

"Fair enough."

"But tell me. What kind of life would you have had?"

"I've been doing my best not to think of it. Not to have to imagine looking across the table at a woman for the rest of my days knowing she only wanted my title and the comfort it provided rather than wanting me."

"So you would have been miserable then?"

"I would have likely posted her in one of the properties I never frequent and gone on about my life as if she didn't exist." It was harsh, and he doubted he would have continued for years on end. But it would have eased his anger for a while at least.

"Would you have taken other lovers?" she asked, quietly. It was too late for him to prepare himself, for when he stared at her, he saw the rush of pink tinge her cheeks. He saw the way her big, green eyes watched him boldly, wanting an answer. He seemed to be stuck in her gaze as she probed his thoughts, looking for the truth. They'd both stopped walking and had turned to face each other.

"That is not proper discussion with a lady," he said, looking away. It was the cowardly way out of the question, but he was glad for it. In truth, he didn't know the answer. He began walking again and she followed. He knew from the soft steps in the sand behind him rather than seeing her. He'd picked up the pace but she had not fallen far behind.

Still, he considered her question.

A vow was a vow. If he promised fidelity, he would want to honor it. But another part of him, perhaps a part similar to Harlow's thirst for revenge, would want to punish the person who'd stolen his chance for a happy life.

"I will remain steadfast, so not to find out," he allowed.

"I'm fortunate for so many brothers on that front, at least."

"How so?"

"They took turns seeing me to balls. Standing guard by my side all night so I'd not be lured into such a trap. Though it does little for one's ego to hear them arguing over who would be forced to do the honor. Often fighting and once even coming to blows over who should have to watch over me. While I didn't appreciate it, I am grateful no fortune-seeking scoundrel was able to trick me into scandal."

"Take care on sharing stories like that, Lady Harlow. For the next time I see your brothers I might need to call them all out for the slight."

She tilted her head and smiled. "I think I should like to see that, my lord." She leaned closer to whisper, "Do not tempt me."

The soft words, with the saucy tilt to her lips, went directly to his cock and had him hard in an instant. Good lord, what this woman did to him without even trying.

HARLOW SAW THE heat in Reese's eyes. It was similar to the night before when he'd been looking at her feet. She'd thought him upset, but now she realized he was tempted. By her.

She was certainly no seductress, being a maiden. But she'd heard her brothers talking when they'd thought she wasn't there. She had some carnal knowledge of what things a man desired in a woman.

Breasts had been the topic of many of their conversations though Harlow didn't understand the appeal. Perhaps it was that women had them exclusively. But a good bit of their time was devoted to discussing a woman's plump backside, and men had those. There seemed to be concern over being able to hold onto a woman for curves were mentioned, specifically as something to hold on to.

She did recall the way seeing a glimpse of a woman's ankle was a signal she was interested in bedsport. They seemed oblivious to the fact that sometimes, completely unintentionally, their ankles were revealed. Be it a deep step or a stiff wind… or walking on the beach as they were now. She didn't want her hems to get wet from the damp sand so she'd picked them up a bit. But she didn't worry for Lord Breckenridge had seen her ankles many times as they settled in the library in the evenings and she'd not intended to send him any messages. She only wanted to be comfortable.

Men were quite silly, she decided. And this secret vocabulary of heated glances and revealing things to mean something else was ridiculous. However had the human race survived this long with such a complex mating ritual? When she was ready to interact in such activities, she planned just to say so.

Except proper young ladies didn't speak of such things. Nor was there any reason for her to need to. For the only time she would ever engage in such acts would be with her husband.

Marriage precipitated the act whether she showed an ankle or not.

But wasn't that rather impractical as well? How would she know if she suited the man or vice versa if they didn't test things between them first? And who were her brothers engaging with if no ladies did this act until married? Statistically it would seem this rule was not strictly followed.

"Forgive me for asking, but have you slept with many women?"

He was in the process of throwing a stick for Belle and her words must have shocked him for the stick landed only a few feet away rather than the great distance he'd been throwing it. Belle cocked her head as if judging his throw and finding him lacking.

But Reese didn't seem to care about the stick for he had turned to her. The heat was gone, replaced by surprise and confusion.

"I don't think that is a subject—"

"Fit for young ladies. Yes, I'm aware. I've heard that so many times. Still, I'm curious. If you don't wish to give numbers, could you tell me, were they ladies of the ton? Because I find fault in the mathematics if every lady be chaste when she marry, but unmarried men are sleeping with ladies. You see the conundrum."

He chuckled.

"My how your mind works, lass. It's intriguing. I would almost love to know the thread of thoughts that trailed to ye asking such a question outright like that."

"You don't intend to answer?" she challenged.

"Very well. Widows." He nearly spat the word at her and looked away as if there was some disgrace in this. But after a few moments of thought she understood. She waited for him to complete his throw before speaking.

"That makes a great deal of sense. They cannot be ruined for they were already married. And one would think after having done the act, one would want to continue doing it. Widowhood is rather sought out by women as it offers a great deal of freedom while also providing funds and safety. Is this widely known by men? I can't think any of my brothers would be clever enough to have thought of this on their own."

He sighed as if he was being put upon to carry a large boulder up a long hill, but eventually answered.

"Aye. Men speak of it in our clubs."

"Which widows are agreeable to such things, you mean?"

"Yes."

"Do you share your preferences for one widow over another?"

"Some men do. I do not." He seemed to gather a great deal of pride in this fact. She didn't know why, but didn't push. She had other questions.

"Because your preferences are different than other men?"

"I would think my preferences are quite common, though I didn't realize how enticing a bold, curious woman could be." He winked.

"If you said that to frighten me so I would stop questioning you, it will not work. I'm rather like a dog with a tasty bone when I want to know something."

"Very well. You have until we get back to the stairs to ask any question you wish and I will answer as to the best of my ability so long as it is not personal. General inquiries only."

Harlow wished she'd been given time to prepare and perhaps a few pieces of paper and some ink, but she'd have to do her best to take advantage of the earl's gracious opportunity.

Reese began to walk for the stairs that would lead them up the cliff to the castle. With his long legs he moved much faster than she could with her shorter ones, but she chased after him as she contemplated what to ask first.

"Have you ever been to a brothel?" she asked because it was something she'd heard about but wasn't quite certain what it was.

"Do you know what that is?" he asked.

"You said I could ask the questions."

"My apologies. Yes. I have."

She bit her bottom lip and then asked, "What is a brothel?"

This earned a laugh and he stopped walking for only a moment.

"It is where men can go to purchase the company of a woman for a set amount of time for a particular purpose. Namely pleasure."

Harlow gasped without wanting to. She didn't want him to think she cast judgment in any way. What he did was not her business.

"And you paid a woman for pleasure?"

"That is a personal question."

She might have argued but she didn't want to waste any time.

"Do the women enjoy it?"

He frowned. "I would guess they do for certain customers, but not all of them."

Harlow swallowed and thought of all the men that overflowed the ballrooms in town and how she would feel if she had to touch them all. Some were quite detestable, while others were not a struggle to look at.

"Have you ever been in love?"

"That is also personal. But no. I thought so, once, but I was mistaken."

"What do men truly want in a woman?"

"That depends on what he wants her for. For marriage, he would likely want a partner. Someone who is witty and would make the harder parts of life easier. Also, she would need to be a good mother to his children. If he was looking for someone to dally with, he would not need to be so choosy. Someone beautiful and eager. That's about all that is necessary."

"Is that why men seem disagreeable to marriage? Because the attributes are in juxtaposition to one another?"

"Are they? I know women who are all the things I mentioned. My friends have already married them. But they do exist."

She nodded.

"What does it feel like? Sexual relations."

The man fairly sprinted the dozen or so feet to the bottom of the stairs, with Belle chasing after him. When he reached the first step, he turned with a bright smile on his face.

"I'm sorry, but the questions are over per our agreement."

"You cheated," she said while shaking her head.

He gasped, "How dare you impugn my honor, my lady."

She rolled her eyes at his theatrics and pointed to the stairs. "Let's go. I'm starving." She had gained a great deal of knowledge on her walk with the earl, but she still had much to learn.

The more she considered it, the more she wanted Reese to be her teacher.

But how?

—◦— ❧ —◦—

# Chapter Thirteen

R EESE MADE HIMSELF too busy after luncheon to join Harlow for their usual afternoon activities. He'd needed some time alone without her on his mind. But as he sat in his study looking over the books and drinking whisky at an ungodly early hour, he was still thinking of her.

He'd grown too comfortable with her, because she'd been here so long. But any day now, his mother should arrive and he could be done with Lady Harlow and all the temptation she had become to him.

She was a danger to his peace of mind, and he'd embraced it rather than wanting her to leave. Surely he was going mad.

When he decided avoiding her wasn't helping, he went to the library to find she was already there, spread out across his settee as she did in the evenings as they read. She'd kicked off her boots and while her feet were tucked demurely under her skirts, he still knew they were there.

Of course, her feet would be attached to her legs under her dress. This kind of thinking was why he was concerned for madness.

"Are you well, my lord?"

He blinked. "Why do you ask?"

"You seem…"

She didn't have a word for what he was either. Perhaps she was too polite to use the word *mad* to describe him.

"Agitated," she finished.

"Agitated?" He played the word across his tongue and found it suited somewhat. She had riled his blood like no other woman had done before.

"Shall we read? Do you wish me to start tonight?" he asked to move things along.

"That would be lovely," she said though she continued to watch him too closely.

As he read the words on the page, he felt her gaze upon him, studying him. He didn't dare look up for to see her with her attention focused on him might be the last strand of his restraint.

He wanted her. Desperately. But she was a maiden, and he'd not debauch a virgin. If she would have agreed to marry him, she'd no longer be a maid.

But she hadn't.

Thea Stonecliff—make that Thea Hayes now—would likely be upset with the disregard with which he was reading her latest book. He read the words in the order they were printed on the page, but that was all he could say for it. For a thousand pounds he couldn't tell anyone what had happened in the last chapter.

When it was Harlow's turn to read, Reese was careful not to touch any part of her hand when he passed the book to her. He'd thought it would be a reprieve, but listening to her soft, smoky voice read to him was just a different form of the same torment.

He wanted her. And he could never have her.

It seemed their bold conversation on the beach today had irreparably broken something between them. He wished to fix it, but what was the point? She would leave to her home soon enough, and next Season she would marry a man of her choosing. She'd have the life she wanted and he would have what he wanted. To be alone.

Except, it was becoming clearer by the minute that was no longer what he wanted.

He wanted her, the thought repeated again, as if hoping for a different answer. But it was the same.

He could never have her.

⟫⟫⟫⟫⟪⟪⟪⟪

WHEN HARLOW HAD read her chapter, she moved to pass the book back to Reese, but he was not paying any attention. It looked as if he was studying the painting on the ceiling. If she was correct it was a depiction of Diana, Goddess of the Hunt, with a falcon on her hand as she rode a stag. Of course, like most portrayals of goddesses, she was bare chested.

Breasts again. Whatever did men find so very appealing about them?

Whether it was the breasts or something else, it was clear the earl was distracted this evening. She'd barely seen him through the day and she wondered if he would join her for their nightly reading. She was almost surprised when he entered the room. Though perhaps she wasn't wrong, for while he was here physically, his mind was somewhere else entirely.

Did he wish her to leave his home? He was a man who enjoyed his peace and quiet. She was a guest who had likely overstayed her welcome. Maybe he'd grown weary of her impertinent questions. She'd gone too far during their walk, but she couldn't bring herself to apologize, even if she should.

"It is your turn, my lord," she said holding out the book for him. He turned toward her and took it but didn't start reading.

"I'm sorry about today," he said.

"What do you mean? You have nothing to apologize for." Her words came out a bit sharp. His regret for a conversation she had so appreciated made her… agitated.

"I should not have allowed the conversation to get so…"

"You mean you wish you would have treated me as every other person in my life. As if I'm too ignorant to learn things about the relations between men and women? I do not accept your apology, for it was all a woman like me could hope for. To have a friend who cared enough to share the information I need. The knowledge I need to go make the best of my life. It is the education all women should have. We are told next to nothing, and yet we're somehow expected to master the act on our first try. I do not accept your apology, but I would ask you to accept my gratitude."

He twisted his lips to one side, as if pondering over what she had said. Eventually he looked up to her face, possibly the first time since they'd come into the library, and smiled.

"You are welcome."

With that he went back to reading his chapter and things felt normal again, when they had previously been uncomfortably strained. Except she should not think of them as being normal. Nothing about this situation was normal or would remain so. She was just a temporary guest in his home. Nothing more.

It could have been different. If she had known him better, she might have seized the moment that first day and had Reese as her own. But how was she to know she would grow to have affections for the earl? How was she supposed to know which suitor she should marry next Season when it would matter most?

When it was her turn to read, she stood to get the book from him.

"Please forgive me," she said out of the blue. She'd been thinking the words for weeks, but hadn't meant to speak them.

"Forgive you? For what?" he asked, seeming baffled as he looked down at the book in his hands. And he was right to be confused, for her words were out of place for their earlier conversation.

She had the opportunity to change course, or brush it off entirely, but she didn't take that route for she'd obviously been thinking about it more than she'd realized.

"I..." She took a deep breath and pushed through. "I apologize for the abruptness of my rejection when you made such a valiant offer of marriage. Or rather made the attempt to offer."

He blinked and cast wide eyes on her. "Do you wish to change your mind?"

She might have laughed at the worry cast in his gaze. She knew he'd rushed to do the right thing without really contemplating what it would mean to take her for his wife, but he'd clearly been grateful she'd refused his suit.

Clearing her throat, she ignored the bit of displeasure at knowing he didn't want to marry her. And she didn't wish to marry anyone who didn't want to marry her. It was at times like this when she wondered if her brothers' taunts that she was spoiled might have had more than a bit of truth to them.

"No. You may rest easy." She frowned when a breath of what could only be relief gusted from his lungs, the sound similar to that first time he'd started to propose. "Perhaps instead of an apology I should say 'you're welcome' for sparing you such a travesty," she fairly snapped.

He chuckled which did nothing to help her sudden irritation with the man.

"I believe you saved us both from something neither of us would have looked upon with much happiness."

That eased her pique slightly for he was placing himself in the same light. But did he really think a life with her would be so bad?

"Perhaps so," she said though she didn't know that she really agreed.

"I'll not say it didn't sting a bit. Mayhap even more than the first time a woman rejected my hand."

This shocked her.

"You proposed to another woman?" she asked. Something cold twisted in her stomach at hearing Reese had wanted to marry another woman, but did little to hide his joy at not having to marry Harlow. It was insulting. She wanted to bring up the numerous proposals she'd turned down so he would see how other men craved her, but that would be petty.

She may very well be jealous, but she wouldn't allow herself to be petty.

"Aye. I mistook her lack of interest in chasing me as honesty and respect. When in truth, the reason she hadn't tried her turn at trapping me was because she was in love with another."

She cleared her throat as she swallowed down her irritation. Perhaps this was the reason he was not seriously interested in her. If he'd given his heart to another and had it broken, he may still be hurting.

"I'm sorry. You must have loved her a great deal."

"What?" he looked over as if just realizing she was still in the room. "No. Not at all."

"I see." So he'd not been burned by love. It seemed both of them spent so much time running away from the possibility someone only wanted them for money or a title that they may have unintentionally avoided the person who was meant for them.

"It was a mistake," he said with a shrug.

"Do you ever think one of the ladies who attempted to trap you might have been someone you could have come to love? Someone who did a bad thing, but for a good reason? Perhaps they cared for you but you paid them no mind so they took matters into their hands in a distasteful way."

He tilted his head as if looking back on the past and shrugged.

"I can't say. Is it something you wonder about all the men your brothers ruled as unsuitable?"

"Yes. I've been thinking about it ever since I woke up on that ship, worried I might die before I had the chance to find the man who was deemed suitable. If I'd died on that ship I wouldn't have known so many things..."

"You will do things differently when you get back to London?"

She nodded and twisted her fingers. "I hope I have that chance."

He reached out and placed his large hand over hers.

"You are safe here, Harlow. I'll not allow anything to happen to you. You have my word."

She trusted him and knew he would protect her. She may never have felt so safe as she did there with him.

"Thank you, but that is not why I worry." It was becoming a habit of telling him more than she meant to. Perhaps it was because of that same trust.

He didn't even ask, he simply tilted his head and she continued to explain.

"After so many years of rejecting every offer of marriage, I'm often ignored or even ridiculed in Society. Men do not waste their time asking me to dance. Women assume I'm too high in the instep and envy the luxury I have to remain unwed while they are forced to find husbands by any means necessary. I have no friends. The ones I had in those first years have long since wed as I've become a spectacle. A lesson to young women on what happens if they are too choosy and don't accept their first offer. I've gone from being the Diamond of the Season to being an unwanted oddity."

"Aye. An oddity indeed." He nodded slowly. "An oddity who is quite skilled in feeling sorry for herself."

She smacked him and laughed as he broke into laugher as well.

"You are a rotter, Lord Breckenridge," she accused playfully.

They laughed a bit more but when their mirth faded into silence, he reached out and placed his hand on hers again.

"Life doesn't always allow us second chances to right a wrong or choose a different path. But from the moment you jumped overboard, you took control of your life again. Don't give it up. Walk into the next ballroom and ask someone you fancy to dance. Get to know him and allow him to know you. Find the person you want, don't wait for him to find you. And please don't rely on your brothers to approve of someone you've come to enjoy."

"That's not how it's done." Though she liked the picture he painted. It seemed easy enough to find a man she could love if she could just ask him how he felt about a variety of topics. But women were expected to speak only on the shallowest of topics. She couldn't tell a prospective gentleman of her fears of growing too old. She was limited to conversations of her skills on the pianoforte and how many children she wished to have.

"Do you care? The old way didn't work. Shouldn't ye try something else?" he asked, challenging her.

She thought over what he'd suggested. It sounded preposterous, but it wasn't as if her reputation as an oddity would be in danger if she acted any more odd. There was some bit of freedom in being the outcast.

Reese was correct that she didn't wish to give up control of her life or the freedom she found in giving up on all the rules.

"I don't give a damn," she said making him smile wide. He was quite lovely. She'd noticed the sturdiness and perfect curves of his form previously, but in this moment she noted the warmth in his brown eyes. "I will ask for what I want, and if I don't get it, I will ask someone else until I find the right man."

"That's a brave lass," he nodded as if he were proud of her.

She didn't realize until that moment that the pride in his eyes was what she'd been fighting for all her life with her brothers and her father. They loved her, she knew that. They indulged her and doted on her, but she'd never known them to ever be proud of her.

Not like Reese seemed to be.

She looked at him again and thought again of what she might have done if he'd had the opportunity to fully ask her to marry him. Would she have kept her promise to herself to marry the next man who asked so she might know what it was like to enjoy the things husbands and wives shared?

She knew well enough a man and woman didn't need to be wed to enjoy those things. And maybe that was what she needed. The chance to know those intimate details with someone she trusted without the pressure of marriage.

It was truly the opposite of everything a young woman is

taught, but she was in control of her fate and this was what she wanted.

"Will you kiss me?" she asked, though her tone made it sound like a challenge.

"You are starting your new plan already?" he asked, but she thought he only wanted to give himself time rather than needing to hear her answer. Or perhaps he was even giving her time to change her mind.

She wasn't about to change her mind. It might have been a rash idea. No. Ideas were things people actually gave thought to. This had not been an idea, it was more of an instinct or a response.

"I am asking you to kiss me, because it's what I want. You are free to say no, and I will find someone else I wish to kiss and ask them. That is how I want to live my life going forward. I don't want to lie in bed, wishing I'd been brave enough to ask. I'm asking. What is your answer?"

# Chapter Fourteen

HARLOW COULD HEAR her heartbeat rushing in her ears and worried she might faint. She'd risked everything to be honest and live her truth in the way he had encouraged her to do. But rather than answer, he only looked at her for so long she considered running from the room.

But eventually she had her answer.

Rather than respond verbally he took a steady breath and leaned down to press his lips to hers.

She'd been kissed before. Her mother placed a kiss to her cheek nearly every night before she went up to her room. Her father often kissed the top of her head, the touch getting lost in her hair. Even her brothers had kissed her on occasion, in celebration of a good prank, or when she'd gotten hurt and they hoped to ease the pain away so Harlow wouldn't tell on them.

She'd seen the way men kissed women they weren't related to. Once when she was younger, she'd snuck up on Luke with a woman in the mews as he'd been practically devouring her face. She'd thought that rather disgusting and not just because one of the participants had been her brother.

The woman seemed to be enjoying it enough to moan and cling to Luke as if wanting more or wanting him to actually devour her. She hadn't understood.

But she thought she understood now.

For she wanted more from Reese. Though unsure what more was, she just knew her body…wanted.

The kiss had started with a mere press of his lips to hers. It shouldn't have caused her mind and thoughts to swim so. He moved his lips together, pulled back just the smallest space. Still so close she doubted a piece of parchment would fit between them, but she felt her body freeze with worry he'd not return.

He did. Repeating the motion from the first touch again and then again. And each time, she became more panicked that that would be the time he wouldn't return.

And then she'd felt his tongue touch inquisitively along the edge of her bottom lip and while she'd always thought a tongue to be a rather rude body part, she used hers to touch his and it somehow wasn't rude, but exquisite. How had she never known her tongue was capable of more than a sharp barb, a taunt, or an apology?

Their tongues started with tender touches and then suddenly his encroached farther into her mouth and she moaned, not unlike that woman in the mews. It was then she realized her hands were clenched in Reese's shirt and she was unwittingly pulling him toward her.

Part of her felt insanely glad her reaction was similar to another woman's. Perhaps she was not so different after all. But a second later, she didn't care if she was the last woman who walked the earth, so long as Reese didn't stop kissing her.

She pressed her body closer to his and felt something hard and hot against her hip that had not been there when their lips first touched. She wasn't sure what it was or where it had come from but she pressed closer and earned a gasp from the man she had suddenly become part of.

They shared the same breath; their hearts raced against one another. It was as if they'd somehow joined together. And the thought of joining together with Reese made her lower body throb with some pleasure she'd never encountered before.

That wasn't true. One night she'd awoken from a dream that a man was touching her between her legs. A shadow with no facial characteristics other than he was a man and he had wanted her.

She'd been frightened initially and then realized she hadn't been afraid of the unknown gentleman. In fact, she'd closed her eyes hoping she could fall back to sleep and pick up the dream where it had left off.

It hadn't.

But now… this was no dream.

"Please," she begged, unsure what exactly she was pleading for. She could only hope Reese knew.

"You asked for a kiss. We must stop, before this turns into far more than a kiss."

She wanted to ask him for whatever this was, but again she didn't know what exactly to ask for. So again, she just said "Please" and held tight to his shirt.

He bent close and took her mouth again, as his hand clasped behind her head, in her hair, holding her to him. His other hand was braced against her lower back, holding that throbbing part of her close to that hard part of him that seemed to lurch against her.

"Please touch me," she asked even though he already was. It just seemed there were other parts of her that needed his touch more than her back and her head. Her nipples had tightened and she wanted him to ease the ache there.

"Harlow," he whispered against her lips. She didn't realize how lovely her name sounded when it was spoken so close to her that she could feel the word rather than hear it.

"Yes. Please, Reese. Please."

"Do you ache?" he asked as if he'd heard her thoughts. "Here?"

His hand had moved across her stomach and she thought he would touch her breasts, but instead his fingers caressed down between her legs.

"Yes," she answered though she was beginning to ache everywhere.

"I will ease the ache, but I can do no more."

She didn't understand what he was saying, but still she answered with, "Yes."

Like a brusque wind, he swept her up and sat her on the settee guiding her to her back as he kissed her lips, her jaw, her neck and then the swell of her bosom cresting her gown.

She repeated the word "yes" more than was likely necessary, but it seemed the only word she remembered with the exception of his name.

Another swift movement later, he was crouched below and her gown had been tugged up. She thought she should cover herself, for this was surely not right, but before that consideration had the chance to hold purchase in her hazy mind, he was touching her in the exact spot she'd wanted him to touch.

She wondered if she'd somehow told him for how else would he know, but then she didn't care for he was kissing her there at the same place he was touching. The two different types of touch caused her to lurch up before pressing closer so he could continue.

She thought she heard a smug chuckle, but didn't care about that either. Nothing mattered but his touching her and not stopping.

With each caress of his tongue and each press of his finger inside her body, she seemed to float higher and higher. Her fingers were clenched in his hair as she tried desperately to catch her breath and then he pressed his tongue harder against a single spot and everything stilled a moment before it burst.

Wave after wave of pleasure so great it was nearly painful crashed around her as her chest heaved and her vision clouded over.

She felt him say something, but she couldn't hear past the rush of her pulse in her ears for some time. And then she felt his breath on her throat, as he placed kisses along her jaw and then her lips. He tasted different, and she realized he must taste like her.

She had been teetering on the edge of exhaustion, but these kisses stirred her anew. She'd not known such pleasure existed. And now she didn't know how she would survive without it.

⫸⫸⫸✕⫷⫷⫷

AFTER BRINGING HARLOW to climax once, he should have stopped. Hell, he should have stopped before he'd even kissed her, but as he could not go back now, the only path was forward and he selfishly wanted to watch her when she took her pleasure this time.

The way she'd grasped tightly to his hair spoke of a passionate woman. He could have guessed as much as Harlow was passionate about other things. Most recently her desire to seek revenge on the man who had hurt her.

Reese could only hope this new situation wouldn't leave her wanting to seek retribution from him as well. He was way beyond the lines of propriety. Being alone together as long as they had was enough to see him married, but this...

He felt the familiar concerns swirling. He should offer for her again, for he'd well and truly ruined her now. It wasn't a matter of circumstance any longer, but a claiming.

Yet, he knew if he asked she would reject him again. For she wanted to choose the man she spent her life with and she wanted a proposal brought about by desire not obligation.

What he wouldn't be able to convince her of was that he truly desired her. Not just this physical sense—though he ached to be inside her body and take her completely—but he desired her in other more important ways. Ways he'd not known he could want a woman.

He wanted these evenings spent curled up together in a cozy room reading to each other and talking about any and every topic that flitted through their minds.

But he'd not ask now. He'd wait until the time was right. Until she could not deny his reasons. Until he was certain she would say yes.

For now, however, he would see her sated so she would know he could satisfy her. His kisses had brought her back to the edge.

She was panting and her green eyes seemed ablaze with lust as he teased her slick folds with his fingertips. It was incredibly powerful, knowing he was the only person who had touched her in this way. Unless…

"Have you ever touched yourself in this way?" he asked quietly.

Her eyes drowsy with desire widened and she shook her head. He could have guessed as much. She wouldn't have known she could, and even then might not have.

Taking her hand in his, he brought her palm to his lips. He kissed softly before teasing his tongue across one of the creases. Then he bit the fleshy part just enough to cause a gasp of surprise.

"I feel like every place on my body is tingling and alive in a way it never has been before."

"Let me show you," he said as he guided her hand down under her skirts. He wished he could remove her clothes entirely but he'd not put her in a state of dishabille that would cause his staff to question.

She shook her head. "I can't."

"When you know you have the power to create these feelings on your own, you'll not need to be so hasty in selecting a man to give them to you," he explained.

She nodded.

He whispered his instructions and she followed each one until she was writhing on his settee, close to orgasm once again. Her quiet whimpers excited him and he pressed his palm against his cock, hoping to ease the pressure.

"Please," she begged as she'd done once before. Christ, how

he loved to hear her beg for him. But she didn't stop with just his name and the quest for more as she had the first time. "Please, Reese. I want to know what it is that a man and a woman do when their bodies come together. Please."

He shook his head. This time the word *please* had wrecked him. He wanted to give in. Needed it. But he couldn't.

He moved back and shook his head.

"I can't, Harlow. Not like this. Not when kissing and touching has taken to flames. I'll not pretend to tell you what you should or shouldn't want. You're a woman grown and I'll not disrespect ye by thinking I know better. But you need to be clear-headed to make such a decision. Not swept away by lust."

She blinked at him as if coming out of a haze. She opened her mouth and he feared she was going to beg him again and it would be their undoing. But whatever she was about to say was interrupted by a sharp knock at the door.

They broke apart and he had her sitting up with her skirts properly at her ankles in a second's time. Her hair, was not any messier than it had been all day.

Only her dazed expression and kiss-swollen lips gave away what they'd been doing and he could do nothing to fix either.

"Yes?" he said with a voice that was much too harsh.

Finch opened the door and peeked just inside.

"Your mother has arrived, my lord."

"Ah. Thank you, Finch." And thank God almighty for such an interruption. "Take her to my study, I will be there momentarily."

When his butler withdrew from the doorway, Reese took yet another step back from Harlow.

"I will go greet my mother and bring her to you in the drawing room for introductions."

"But I am a mess," she said looking down at her body.

"You may feel as such, as if everything has changed, but I assure you, you look the same. Well, nearly." He brushed a finger over her bottom lip. "You are somehow more beautiful than you were."

She blinked and shook her head. "I've no need for your flirting. Go see your mother as I shake away the cobwebs from my brain."

He chuckled and with a nod, he quit the room as quickly as he was able without running.

His mother had come not a minute too soon.

# Chapter Fifteen

HARLOW STARED AT the place where Reese had left the room to go see his mother. As if he had been unaffected by what had happened between them.

On legs that felt much too wobbly to hold her, she made her way down the hall to the drawing room. She settled into a chair and opened the book, hoping it looked as if she'd been alone in that room for some time.

Her heart still hammered in her chest as she tried to relax and look like her world had not been tilted on its axis moments before. Had she begged Reese to take her virtue?

Yes, she had. Perhaps he'd been right to make her wait until her head had lifted from the fog of longing. But even now, clearheaded and downright frightened to be called out for what happened, there was still a desire to be with Reese in that way.

He'd thought she would change her mind when she was not heated with lust, but she still wanted him. She wanted to see him naked. She wanted to explore his body and touch him. See what he looked like when he took his pleasure.

He had touched her and had her touch herself. He'd has his mouth… She should be embarrassed. But she wanted more. She wanted everything with him.

And now he was going to bring his mother in here to introduce them.

Harlow was certain the woman would take one look at her and know exactly what had transpired minutes before.

Was Harlow's hair under control? Were her cheeks flushed? She heard footsteps approaching and looked about the room desperate for a place to hide, but it was too late. The door opened and Reese held out his arm for a small blonde woman to enter before him.

"Mother, this is Lady Harlow Haverston, daughter of the Duke and Duchess Ar—"

"Ardmere, yes. I know your mother well. You are the very image of her."

Harlow didn't know how well acquainted the women could be as she'd never known Lady Breckenridge to visit their home, but she smiled.

Harlow was pleased to be said to look like her mother, for she thought her mother to be quite beautiful. She certainly was when she smiled. She had a number of dimples that Harlow lacked.

But most of all, Harlow was just glad the woman had not pointed at her and called her a harlot.

"It is a pleasure to meet you Lady Breckenridge. Thank you so much for coming to aid in the preservation of my reputation."

"Yes, well, I was not given a choice in the matter, but I hope to be of some assistance. I understand you have been here all this time unattended," the woman said shrewdly as Harlow tried to keep her breathing even. That feeling of wanting to dart away like a rabbit being chased by a wolf had returned.

"As I mentioned, Mother, it was through no fault of Lady Harlow or myself that we have come to be in this situation. Your statement that nothing untoward has transpired will serve to assure all those interested that Lady Harlow has not been compromised."

"As you say. But I am being told to put my good name on the line when I know not what has happened in all these weeks you were alone. The best thing for everyone would be for the two of you to be wed. Then there could be no question on the matter."

Harlow could not look at Reese. To see the horror he must be feeling would hurt her more than she realized. She thought she might be ill. She didn't want Reese to be forced into marrying her. Not when he'd helped her and offered every kindness. She knew he didn't want to marry under such conditions and to be the one forced upon him… She'd not been like those women who had tried to trap him but the result would be the same. No.

"I assure you, Lady Breckenridge, your honorable son has already offered, and while I'm touched by the gesture, it is entirely unnecessary for him to make such a sacrifice. Besides, nothing untoward has happened."

She silently sent out a thought of gratitude to her brothers and all the schemes that had resulted in them being able to lie so effortlessly. The skill had grown rusty with disuse, but enough remained to get her out of this difficulty.

"I take it you declined his offer of marriage?" the lady said with an unhappy tilt to her head. Was she upset she couldn't force her son into marriage or put out with Harlow for rejecting her child. Harlow couldn't tell and this whole matter was growing tedious.

"I will deal with the consequences if you are unable to vouch for our propriety."

Lady Breckenridge let out a sigh and turned toward her son. The man Harlow had yet gathered the courage to look at.

"I am beginning to think the only way you may ever marry is if you are caught in your altogether with a woman. You slip through the parson's noose much too easily."

"After your deceit, I feel you owe me this reprieve, Mother. You will tell all that you have served as chaperone and, in fact, you invited Lady Harlow to Slains Castle."

"My, such an elaborate ruse. It makes one wonder what has really happened."

"So long as one tells everyone what one is instructed to say, one may have the funds to purchase a new gown before the next Season."

Harlow barely followed all of that but it was clear Reese was daring her to try him.

"Threats, love? Hmm…" She raised her brows and Harlow couldn't help but compare the countess to that of a cat toying with a mouse. "Very well. I will assume everything was above board in the time I've been away, and I will do my duty as chaperone to watch over the lady as I should. But know this, if I learn of anything untoward having happened, I will insist upon a wedding. I know you are put out by my machinations during the Season, but you have a duty to produce an heir so the Breckenridge title continues into succession. Do not blame me if I've grown tired of waiting for you to see to it."

With that, the woman turned and paused at the door.

"I am tired from my travels. I will retire to my room and see you both for dinner."

When the woman was gone, Harlow risked a glance at Reese who was still looking after the wake of the formidable woman. He turned back to Harlow and let out a breath.

"What happened here before she arrived cannot happen again." And then he turned in much the same way as his mother had, and quit the room, leaving Harlow standing there alone.

⤜⤛⤚⤙

REESE SLUMPED IN his chair behind the heavy desk in his study and poured himself a third glass of whisky. The first two had done little to stop thoughts of Harlow from taunting him.

He imagined since the lass was destined to stay at Slain's until their ruse was played out, he would need to find a better way to deal with the temptation she posed. Drinking himself into a stupor day after day wasn't a viable plan.

Reese had been with many lovely women over the years. But

he'd never spoiled a maid. Harlow hadn't been his for the taking, but while he'd thought himself an honorable man, he doubted a monk could have turned away a woman as lovely as she.

When she'd looked up at him with those green eyes filled with lust, he'd nearly come undone with his clothes still on.

He was rather proud of himself that he'd not succumbed. He'd protected her, as well as himself. For if he'd given in, he surely would have found himself on the wrong side of the marriage alter.

Although now he wasn't sure which side that was. He should have been pleased that she'd stopped his mother from pressing them into a union, but a part of him wished she would have agreed.

It was cowardly of him. He wanted her without the risk of rejection. But clearly he'd been right. If he'd asked for her hand, she would have turned him down. Again.

She'd seen reason once her blood had cooled, and he was sure she would be grateful he'd turned her away. And now that his mother had arrived, he and Harlow would be safe from any further entanglements.

Setting the glass aside, he stood and checked his legs before heading into the dining room. His mother was already seated at the opposite end of the table from his seat.

He glanced to the chair next to his where Harlow had sat previously. Would she sit next to him tonight? Or would she sit next to his mother? Surely down there away from him was best.

As soon as he was seated, a footman came to set a napkin across his lap as another began serving.

"Shouldn't we wait for Lo—Lady Haverston?"

"The lady has requested a tray be brought to her room, my lord," Elkins reported as he held a dish for the woman at the end of the table.

"I see. She's been tormented by megrims since washing ashore. It's not uncommon for her to take her meals in her room," Reese said for his mother's benefit, even if it had only been true in the early days of Harlow's arrival, when she was anchored to her bed chamber because of her sore ankle.

Still his mother didn't need to know the specifics and his staff would never speak against him. It would help prove to his mother that they were nothing but the epitome of innocence all these weeks.

"I will check in on her after our meal," his mother said.

"Thank you, Mother."

He nodded, but his lips were pressed too tightly together to offer a smile. For if his mother had not arrived, he would be free to check on Harlow himself. Now he must let it be up to someone else while he worried about her.

Why had he written for his mother?

He shook his head. No. This was better. He could not be tempted into ruining anyone if his mother was in attendance. Doing anything with Harlow would be too great a risk.

The meal seemed to drag out and he found he wasn't so very hungry. Possibly because his belly was filled with an adequate supply of whisky already. But he was glad when his mother dabbed at her mouth with her napkin and nodded to the footman to help her stand.

"You'll report back if it is more than a megrim and I will call for a doctor," Reese said as his mother made for the door.

"Of course."

He waited for nearly an hour before assuming all was well and the lass didn't require medical attention. Or his attention.

As he traveled up to his room, he found he missed Harlow, despite having seen her just hours earlier.

However, this distance was for the best. In fact, if he didn't see Harlow until her family arrived, that would solve all his problems.

But he soon realized as he removed his cravat and shirt the temptation remained. For he wanted her as much as he had before. He found himself remembering every detail. The way her skin felt against him. The scent of her. The softness of her hair.

Shaking his head, he tried again to dispel the memories. For Harlow Haverston didn't wish to marry him. She would never be his.

⚜

# Chapter Sixteen

HARLOW HOPED SHE'D done an adequate job of hiding her disappointment when she opened her door to find Lady Breckenridge rather than her son.

After they'd gone their separate ways, Harlow had grown weary and returned to her room to ready for dinner. But when the time came to descend the stairs, she couldn't do it.

She didn't want to sit with them at dinner, making polite conversation and spewing more lies. Lies she feared the woman might see through if Harlow was not on guard the entire meal.

She could only feign their innocence for so long when what she was really thinking was how she might pull Reese into a dark room and kiss him again. No, it was better if she hid away and took her meal in her room where it was safe.

"We missed you at dinner, my dear. Are you well? The earl stated you've had megrims quite often since you arrived."

Harlow smiled at the way the woman made it sound as if she'd arrived in a carriage instead of spat out on the shore by the sea.

"That is true. After being hit on the head, it has bothered me. But it is not as bad as it once was. Originally I could hardly stand the light."

The woman nodded.

"It was lucky my son was at home to aid in your recovery."

"Yes," Harlow said carefully wondering if it was a trap. This was the very reason why she hadn't gone down to dinner.

"I don't recall you being betrothed."

"Pardon?"

"You turned down my son's offer. I can only think you would do so if you were already engaged."

"No, my lady. I am not engaged. It is just that I know Re— Lord Breckenridge does not wish to marry."

The woman's brow rose at Harlow's near slip before she let out an unladylike sound and waved. "The lad is stubborn is all. He doesn't know what he wants."

Harlow winced at this and shook her head.

"No. He's a man. And while he made an offer to be honorable, it was clear he wishes to marry only when he is free to do so. Not out of duty or obligation. And, I would say, I agree. I've turned away many suitors already. Men who wanted my dowry without a thought for me."

"It is a luxury many do not have to be choosy." She raised her blonde eyebrows at Harlow.

"I understand. And I realize now, that perhaps I relied on other opinions too often. Still, I will accept a man I can consider a friend and partner."

"I see." She let out a breath and turned for the door. "I'll leave you to your rest. I hope your megrim subsides by morning. You and I will be spending a great deal of time together. I do hope you like embroidery." Somehow the woman had made it sound like a threat.

After Harlow had assured Lady Breckenridge she was in good health and looked forward to seeing her in the morning, the woman patted Harlow's hand and left the room. Harlow waited a moment before she peered out in the hall to see what room the woman had gone to. She saw the door at the far end of the hall close and returned to her own room.

Harlow changed for bed and then lay there looking up at the

canopy above her for the next hour. For as tired as she'd been earlier, she didn't feel the faintest hint of fatigue now.

She tossed to her other side as her mind whirled with thoughts of kissing Reese and the way he'd touched her. He'd shown her how to touch herself to bring about her own pleasure, but she knew it would be a poor substitute for the man she wanted in her arms.

She appreciated that he'd stopped them before anything had happened. She understood why he'd done as much. He'd been right, she'd not been thinking clearly. Her mind had been muddled with desire.

He'd trusted her to know her own mind, but wanted her to be sure. Now, here alone, with her body cooled—or at least not as heated—she found she still wanted him just as much as she had that afternoon.

Of course, if they'd proceeded earlier, they would have certainly been caught by his mother when she'd arrived.

Harlow knew having a chaperone would be important in sparing what was left of her reputation. It meant she would be able to return to London next year and be accepted in Society.

There, she might meet a man who would become her husband and the father to her children. But that seemed so long from now. And she'd waited so long already, she didn't want to wait anymore.

Reese had awakened feelings in her she wanted to explore. Things having his mother here had put an end to before Harlow was ready.

The older woman seemed intent on marrying them off so they would need to be careful. If she so much as caught them looking at each other with passion in their gaze, they would likely find themselves in front of a blacksmith. At least that's the way Harlow had heard they did things in Scotland.

Perhaps it was best if they kept their distance from each other so not to get caught. Disinterest would help to convince the countess there was nothing between them.

Not that there was anything between them. Except, she found she very much wanted there to be. Once she'd decided on her plan, she hopped out of bed eager to set it in motion.

Opening her door, she looked to her left. Harlow wondered if the countess usually stayed at the opposite end of the hall from her son, or if Reese had done that for some other purpose. Maybe that slight hostility between them was more serious than she'd thought.

Harlow would figure that out later. All that mattered now was that the woman would be far enough away that she wouldn't hear Harlow leaving her room and heading in the opposite direction.

Harlow winced and froze when her door squeaked upon opening wider. After a few seconds when nothing happened, she continued on her way.

Wiping her damp palms on her dressing gown, she padded silently down the hall to the room she knew belonged to the earl.

Listening at the door, she waited making sure she didn't hear him speaking to his valet, and then she tapped lightly, the sound so much louder in her mind that it probably was. In fact, it must have been too quiet for it seemed he'd not even heard it.

She knocked again a little firmer and a few seconds later the door opened.

Reese stood before her in only his breeches with his braces hanging at his hips. His chest was bare and she noticed the slight bit of gold hair between flat, brown nipples.

She looked up into his brown eyes and her mouth fell open.

"What's wrong?" he asked as he looked past her into the hall. Surely, he must think the castle was ablaze. For what else would have brought her to his door in the middle of the night?

"Might I come in?" she asked, doing her best to sound sure.

He tilted his head as if trying to puzzle out her motives. She wished him luck in that for she hadn't figured it out yet, and she had the advantage of hearing her own thoughts. Though her thoughts were quite a muddle at the moment so maybe that was no benefit.

"Your head?" he asked. "My mother said she would call for me if you needed a doctor."

"My head is fine. In fact, I only stayed in my room because I didn't know how I might sit in the room with you."

He frowned, but eventually stood aside so she could enter. He then shut the door behind her.

"You're angry with me. About what happened. I can't tell you—"

"No. I'm not angry," she said quickly, but she didn't share anything else.

Now that she was there in his room she had no idea what to do next. She looked about with her hands linked causally behind her back as if it was no more than a visit to see the color of his walls and what trinkets lay out on his dressing table.

The answer: blue, and his table held only a watch fob and a comb.

She needed to think of something clever to say. Or perhaps, if clever was beyond her, she might try seduction.

The idea nearly brought a round of laughter to her lips for she'd never attempted such a thing before and had no clue as to how to progress.

She'd seen the women in the ballrooms, the way they'd fluttered their fans and looked down demurely. She had no fan, but perhaps she would try the looking down bit.

She cast her eyes down and noticed his feet were bare. In the dim light of the room she noticed the slightest of blond hair on his toes. Of course, she knew men had hair on their toes. She'd grown up with five examples. But her brothers, all dark-haired like her, were quite different.

Why did seeing his feet send a shock of warmth through her body to pool in her stomach? It was an intimacy she could imagine no other woman had ever seen. She was not so foolish to think she was the only one. He was a worldly man. She'd seen evidence of it in the way he'd kissed her and the devilish grin he'd given her on occasion.

"Your toes…" God, why had she said that out loud? If there could be something further from seduction, mentioning a man's toes must be it.

"Aye. I've ten of them." He wiggled them. "Just like most people." He waited a moment longer before asking. "Did you come here to make sure?"

"No, of course not." But she was still looking at them as her face flushed hot. She couldn't bring herself to look up at him now. She might have fled the room but she was not one for giving up on something she'd set her mind on doing.

"Would it be rude of me to ask why you have come to my room at such a late hour?"

"It wouldn't be rude. It would be quite understandable in fact, though I don't wish to share the answer."

"I see, so it's to be a game then? I'm to guess? What do I win if I get it right?"

She heard a smile in his voice and it helped in easing her embarrassment, but she still couldn't bring herself to look him in the eye.

"Very well, I'll assume I'm to name my prize if I guess correctly. Let's see…"

He moved as if walking in a circle around her.

"You don't seem to be frantic with fear so I'll not guess that the castle is aflame. Nor will I guess the roof has collapsed as you don't seem to be covered in plaster. Your dressing gown is not wet, so there's been no flood. I do believe I can rule out any grand disaster."

She risked a glance up at him to see he was looking up at the ceiling while tapping his chin. She smiled or would have if she didn't press her lips firmly together to keep it from escaping.

"I don't think it could be a spider for you grew up with five brothers so you are probably less afraid of the furry beasts than I am."

This was true enough. While she didn't like them she'd managed not to scream when in their presence for it would only have meant they'd have been used against her.

"There are a fair number of books in your room so if the issue was that you couldn't sleep you could have entertained yourself for months with the materials available. You're too old to need soothing from a nightmare. And you're clearly awake, so you're not sleep walking."

He'd come to stand directly in front of her again. She knew because his toes were inches away from her own bare toes that were peeking out from under her night rail.

"I can only surmise you've come to seduce me."

Her head snapped up and she looked into his eyes for the first time since she'd entered the room. He was smiling but as his gaze appeared to flick over her face his smile faded.

"Oh dear, I'd said it as a jest, but... surely that can't be it." He shook his head. "We agreed not to pursue what happened earlier. We can't... I won't..."

She'd been so brave in her room, when she'd decided this was something she'd wanted to do. She hadn't even considered that he might reject her. She'd always been told men would go to great lengths to take a woman to their bed, she'd thought Reese would jump at the opportunity. What a fool she'd been.

And worse she couldn't force her legs to carry her away from this humiliation. Instead, as she stood there looking at him, tears began to well in her eyes. This was even worse than running away. Dear Lord, her chin had started to tremble too.

Run! She implored herself but she was stuck there as if frozen except she'd never felt her skin so hot. Not even the time she'd spend too much time swimming in the sun and had turned the shade of a beet.

"Harlow?" he whispered and she saw his throat move when he swallowed. "Tell me why you are here. And why you were smiling and now you're crying. What have I done?"

She wiped the tears away brusquely and shook her head.

"I'm so sorry. I don't know what I was thinking," she managed to say. "Of course, you would not want… That is, you likely prefer women who know their way…" When she gestured toward the bed, she wished the castle *was* on fire for flames might serve to cool her scorched flesh.

This afternoon had only been a brief misstep for him, while to her it had been everything she'd never known she wanted.

"Harlow," he whispered her name and she looked away from his pity.

"I should go, yes? Yes, of course, I should go. I shouldn't have come in the first place. How silly you must think me, just showing up in your room and staring at your feet." *Christ, Harlow, stop mentioning the man's toes.* "I will leave you alone."

Her legs moved clumsily like she were made of iron and had rusted stiff. But at least she was moving. One step followed by another. Her vision had gone sparkly around the edges like the surface of a pond in the sunlight. Was she going to swoon? Please let her stave it off until she was alone in the hall at least.

Her fingers reached out for the door, but she was intercepted by his hand, large and warm. He held hers to his bare chest which was somehow hotter than her hand.

"Wait. Please."

She stood there looking at the place where the back of her hand rested against his skin, but he didn't say anything for a drawn-out minute as her heart raced.

"Your toes," he said.

She looked up at him to see if he was mocking her but his gaze seemed fixed on her feet. She wiggled them as he'd done.

"I've ten of them also," she said.

As he raised his head to look at her, the earlier embarrassment faded, leaving her stomach to flip and twist around.

"Harlow, please tell me if you are not here to seduce me before I kiss you, for once I give in I may not be able to stop."

"You said I couldn't have more when I was heated from kissing. I needed to be of rational thought, and I am—or rather I was. I did come here to seduce you, but only realized when I arrived that I don't know how it is done."

"Are you certain? I promised to be a gentleman, and now I'm a breath away from betraying that vow."

"It's strange, but knowing I could have died on that ship, or perhaps faced something worse than death, it has changed the way I look at things. I don't want to risk not having the chance to live. I know I'm safe, but I still want this. With you. I'm certa—"

Her words were cut off when his lips slammed down on hers.

# Chapter Seventeen

REESE PULLED BACK slightly from their kiss and looked her in the eye. He needed to be sure.

"Once we do this, you will no longer be a virgin."

"I know."

"It might hurt." He'd never deflowered a virgin, but that was common knowledge.

"I'm aware. I'm ready."

"How can you be ready when you don't know what it will be like?"

She smiled and shook her head.

"I'm ready to find out what it will be like."

"You're sure, Lo? For if you regret it, I will likely fling myself over the cliff to the sea."

"So dramatic," she chided before kissing his throat. She pulled away. "Can Belle come live with me if you throw yourself into the sea?"

"You are horrid," he teased with his words as he fingers teased her nipple through her thin night gown. "You could pretend to be distraught over my concerns."

"I know my own mind, Reese and I want this. I want you."

Those were the words he'd been dreaming of hearing her speak. He'd not try to dissuade her again. And not only because he didn't want to. But because Harlow was not a spoiled princess giving into a selfish whim.

She'd gained perspective from her brush with death and he knew from his own experience how it made people want more from life than they'd had. This was what she wanted and he would make sure she was not disappointed.

He kissed her again and again, surprised by how much he enjoyed it. Kissing had always been nothing more than a precursor to the next step. The better step. But kissing Harlow was more than that. He, of course, wanted to do more with her, but if she'd not wanted anything more than kissing, he would have been eager to spend the night with nothing but his lips and tongue touching hers.

Her breathing had picked up and the green in her eyes had gone vibrant with lust as he slipped her night rail off and looked down at her body.

He'd known she was beautiful, but seeing her like this with the candlelight touching her curves, he thought her a goddess sent from the heavens just for him.

His hands fit her body perfectly. Her breast filled his palm, as he explored it thoroughly with his mouth.

She groaned softly and the sound set him ablaze. He wanted to remove the restriction of his breeches, but he knew to do so would send him into a frenzy and he wanted to take his time. Instead, he adjusted his frustrated cock.

Harlow must have noticed his discomfort for she pulled away to look at the very place the fabric did little to hide. She reached out and placed her small hand on the bulge, causing him to gasp with surprise. His body lurched out at her of its own accord.

Rather than pull her hand away, she wrapped her fingers around him, turning his gasp into a moan. If he was not careful, he would spend from just her touch through his breeches.

Reaching down, he gently pulled her hand away.

"You do not like to be touched there?" she guessed incorrectly.

"Oh aye, I like it too well. But if you continue touching me like that, I'll not be able to do all the things to you I've been dreaming of. And that would be a travesty."

"I don't know what you mean by that, but if it keeps you from speaking of throwing yourself in the sea again, I shall stop."

He chuckled, enjoying her humor even in such a serious moment. He could easily see himself spending his days happy with her. For now, he had tonight. And he would make it perfect for her.

⟫⟪

HARLOW'S HEART WAS racing. She didn't think she'd ever been so nervous or excited in her life. All the antics she'd gotten up to with her brothers were nothing compared to this feeling.

Reese had kissed her until she worried she might go mad, and then he'd abandoned her lips only to torment all the other parts of her body. Her neck, her breasts, her ribs, and hips. Even the spot behind her knees seemed wrought with pleasure and she knew she'd never had such an issue in that place before for she'd touched it many times.

It was him. Reese. He seemed an illusionist for when he touched her, it felt like every body part was directly connected to the throbbing place between her legs. It was mystifying.

Eventually when she began to sway and worry she'd fall over, he swept her up into his arms and carried her to his large bed. When he placed her down on the mattress, he followed her down. His hot body pressed against hers.

Instinctively, she raised her legs on either side of his slim hips and the movement allowed him to press closer to the place she wanted him most. She felt that hard ridge in his trousers against the soft warmth of her body.

"Please," she said. My but this man brought her to begging much too easily, but she couldn't care at the moment for he'd retreated. "No."

She reached for him, wanting to bring him back to her, but he reached down for the falls of his breeches and she realized he was going to remove the rest of his clothes.

Since she very much wanted to see more of his body, she let him go. He stood and stripped away the fabric, revealing a body part she'd never seen before.

She understood this part of him would go inside of her, but she wasn't sure of the how of it or even the where. She would have to trust him to show her.

He returned to bed, his warm weight pressing her down in a wonderful way. That part of him lurched against the inside of her thigh, rousing her to lift her hips in welcome.

And then he touched her… there. Not with his fingers or his mouth, as he'd done before, but with… it. She felt a fool for not knowing the proper words for their body parts, but such things weren't often shared with maids. She would ask Reese and he would tell her. But not now.

Now she didn't wish for him to be distracted by anything.

"More," she said. It seemed she was reduced to only two words. More and please. Oh, and his name, which he seemed to enjoy hearing her say. There was no earl, or Lord Breckenridge, this evening. He was Reese.

"Are you ready?" he asked.

She nodded, though there was no real way for him to know for sure if she were ready. As he'd pointed, out she didn't know anything. But she desperately wanted to.

"Yes," she said, hoping it would move him along.

She was not disappointed when he reached between them, grasping himself and rubbing that hot part of him against her.

Her eyes fell closed from the pleasure as he continued for a few moments. Then he adjusted himself over her and pressed slightly. So this was where he would enter her body.

While it felt right in many ways, it also felt somewhat impossible. For his fingers had been inside her there and it had stretched her in a pleasant way. This part of him was much larger than his fingers.

"This will work?" she asked, wanting him to assure her.

"Yes. It will. And it will be wonderful. I promise."

She nodded, trusting him completely. With a sudden thrust, he was inside her. She gasped this time with the pain of it. She blinked in confusion for she'd been in the throes of pleasure one moment and now that was all gone, replaced by pain.

She shifted to get away and he pulled back slightly, but the burn relented only a fraction.

"I'm sorry, I hurt ye," he said. "I thought getting that part over with quickly would be best."

She wanted to tell him how wrong he'd been, but then she recalled hearing that losing one's virginity caused pain. He'd mentioned as much before they began and she'd assured him she was aware.

And even as she was thinking she'd not been prepared for this amount of pain, the sting faded. When he pressed in again, it didn't hurt as bad and by the fourth or fifth time the pain had relented and that warm throbbing had returned.

He continued to move slowly, until her body became unhappy with his pace and began to rock up to meet his.

He smiled down at her. "Is it better now?"

"Yes. The pain is gone now."

"Good, then we can do better than this."

When she opened her mouth to ask what he meant, he kissed her, his tongue taking advantage. He held tight to her as he began to move faster, each thrust coming quicker than the one before.

She didn't stop her movements to meet his every push into her body. When before she'd worried he'd never fit inside her, now she only wanted him deeper. And faster.

With each press of his body she felt herself being pulled closer and closer to that place she'd only learned about hours before. And then she was soaring.

It was even better than it had been before because at the same time her body pulsed, his body spasmed, sending a heat deep into her body.

This man had changed her forever. He'd worried she would have regrets, but there were none. There never could be.

## Chapter Eighteen

"WHY DO YOU not try to do that as much as possible?" Harlow asked him when they had caught their breath. Reese chuckled, loving the way her mind worked. And her brazenness to ask any question that popped into her beautiful head.

"In truth, I do try to do it as much as possible, but it is not an easy thing."

"Why not?"

"Ye remember we talked about the math?"

"Yes. Widows."

"Correct. But there are not so many widows available for as many men in London."

"I see." She couldn't but he would remedy that. He wanted to share everything with her. It wasn't right that young women went about ignorant of the world around them. Harlow had wanted to learn and he would be happy to teach her.

"Widows are not the only option."

"Brothels."

"Aye, where there is pleasure there is a man is willing to pay for it. But there are risks in such establishments."

"Risks?"

"Diseases the like you should never need to see. The women,

while eager for coin, are not always eager for sport. They pretend and skilled actresses they are not. So it feels… contrived."

She frowned. "I can't imagine not wanting to do that. But I guess if I didn't have a say as to who I was doing it with, it would change my perspective."

She was a smart lass.

"A man who doesn't want to share a woman with others can get himself a mistress."

"I believe James had a mistress last season. I heard David and Luke lecturing him about it. They said she was too expensive."

"Yes. Mistresses generally insist on having a place of their own and enjoy expensive gifts. They search for protection from a man who can never take them to wife."

"So they seek rich men, which limits their options."

"Correct. They are better actresses, but are just a different version of the first."

"Hmm."

"Some men will turn to their staff, though I never would. Other men prey on virgins and manage to steal a lady's virtue without becoming embroiled in scandal."

Harlow's eyes went wide and he thought maybe this wasn't the best conversation to have, but she wanted to know. And he'd give her anything she asked.

"Both of those options are disreputable but not the least honorable." He'd not speak of it. Especially when it might have been her fate aboard the Zephyr.

"You mean men who simply take what is not freely given."

"Yes." He let out a breath and turned the topic to lighter subjects. Her favorite studies as a school girl. Her favorite foods.

"And what of your favorite time of year?" he asked his next question, fascinated to learn everything about her.

"I would say winter."

"Truly?" Her answers never failed to surprise him.

"Yes. It is the time of year everyone is expected to stay in-doors and find their own quiet entertainments. Like reading alone in my room. Plus there is Christmastide, and who doesn't like receiving sweets?"

"I shall remember that," he said. "Should I bring you sweets when you return home? I should like to call on ye."

"I would rather other things than sweets, my lord," she said with a naughty tilt to her smile. She may not have come to his room knowing how to seduce a man, but she had gained the skill in the time she was in his bed.

She kissed him and as was becoming common, they were instantly swept away.

"Are you sore, lass?" he asked, knowing he might have to wait until she was ready for him again.

She shook her head and tried to pull him over on top of her, but he was ready to show her something else. Instead he rolled to his back and pulled her up to sit on him.

She looked about in confusion and then the slipped his hand between them to settle his cock against her.

"Oh," she said in some surprise.

"You can determine our pace this time."

Her green eyes lit up with understanding and she smiled her lioness grin.

Soon enough she was moving much too fast for his self-control. He did his best to warn her and when that didn't work he simply held on as best he could. When he felt her squeezing him tightly, he gave in with a growl.

She collapsed on top of him, their hearts pounding against each other. When his body slipped from hers, she giggled as if it tickled and he smiled and kissed her hair.

"I must apologize if I fall asleep. It has been a long day and all of our efforts have drained me completely," he admitted for she was likely to kill him if she attempted to rouse him again.

"I feel the same way, yet I don't wish this night to end."

He agreed. He didn't know what she would have tomorrow or the next. She'd wanted only to know what happened between a man and a woman and now she did. She wanted to live a life that she'd worried she wouldn't have.

He'd known that same fear once.

That night when he'd been shot. As he'd heard the other agents calling out for help and hustling him off to a surgeon, he'd been in and out of consciousness. And in those areas between, he'd thought strange things. His mind seemed to provide all the things he'd never had the chance to experience.

How he'd never taken a sea voyage. Not that it was something he wished to do now as he lost his stomach when aboard a boat for any length of time.

He also thought of more personal matters. He'd never felt the joy of holding his child in his arms. Something he hoped to avoid for some time. He remembered thinking how he'd never loved a woman.

He thought maybe he was beginning to know what that felt like.

"I UNDERSTAND," REESE said into the quiet that surrounded them. Harlow had begun to doze off while thinking all sorts of random things, but now she worried he'd been speaking and she'd only heard that one thing. When he continued, she realized he'd been lying there allowing his mind to wander as she had.

"That is, before when you said you felt different after getting off the ship as if you wished to live and didn't want to miss out on things. I understand."

"You were also taken hostage on a ship full of men who wished to do you harm and chose to plummet into the ocean rather than face living at their hands?"

She'd meant it to be a jest, but he turned to look at her with a frown.

"I don't know if I told you how brave that was."

"It wasn't foolish?"

"Perhaps a little, but let's go with brave for now." He brushed a finger through her hair and the slightest touch seemed to wake her desire yet again. She hadn't realized once it was released it would never be put back in its cage.

"What I meant was that I understand that feeling. Like you may not live long enough to do the things you wished to do."

It was her turn to frown.

"What happened?"

He simply shook his head.

"It doesn't matter now. I lived through it. But instead of doing those things I thought I would miss out on had I died, I've fallen back into the same old life I had before. Even knowing it could all be over in the blink of an eye, hasn't forced me to experience all of those things I would miss. I don't know if I could be any more ungrateful."

She placed her palm against his cheek.

"That's the thing with living, isn't it? That you have time to try things again and again."

"I imagine so. Mayhap with you here, I'll be more inclined to live."

"Well, I have enjoyed living in your bed, but I grow tired and I'm afraid to fall asleep here for we could be found out."

"Would that be so bad?" he asked quietly.

She turned to look at him but he only looked away. For a man who had barely escaped the Season without being shackled to a wife, this surprised her.

"Neither of us should be forced into a marriage simply because we chose to live."

He nodded. "You're right," he said, though he didn't look as if he actually agreed. Before she could question him further, he smiled. "Very well. I will see you to your room."

She tied the sash at her waist and shook her head.

"It's clear I know the way. I managed to find your room on my own, I'll find my way back easy enough."

"It's the polite thing to do. Just because I'm a Scot doesn't mean I'm a barbarian. Despite what you young ladies are taught." He winked and moved for the door.

"Perhaps, but if we're found wandering the halls at this late hour together there would be questions. If I'm found alone, I can easily say I had trouble sleeping and went to the library for a book to read." Was this the first time he'd ever had to sneak around in the middle of the night?

She and her brothers had done it far too often as they played pranks on one another. It was not uncommon to have slipped into one of her brother's rooms only to find it empty because they were out doing the same thing to her or a different brother.

God bless her parents. Whyever had they had so many children?

"I believe I should only like one child, so I might keep track of them easier," she blurted without thinking.

His eyes went wide and he shook his head. "I took precautions so there will be no children."

"I don't mean with you. I meant when I marry, next Season." The Season would be over by the time her family arrived and her uncle paid for what he'd done. She would need to wait until next year for the chance to find a suitable man to wed. But at least she would now know what awaited her in her marriage bed. Thanks to this man.

She stood on tiptoe to place a kiss on the edge of his mouth.

"Thank you," she said.

"I believe I should be thanking you. It was an extravagant gift you bestowed upon me this evening. I hope you don't come to regret the loss."

"I don't feel as if I've lost anything. In fact, I feel I have gained so much in the last hours. I'm grateful, Reese. And no matter who I marry next year, I will always think back on this night with you with great fondness."

With that she kissed him once more and hurried down the hall to her room.

As she crawled into her bed, she felt pleasantly sore in the majority of her body. She was ready to drift away and dream of the husband she would have one day.

But like before, she couldn't quite fall asleep. For all of her thoughts of a husband were filled with visions of Reese. She imagined it was because she'd just been with him and she didn't have another face to put in his place at the moment.

But as she considered, she found envisioning Reese as her husband was not so bad at all. In fact, it was rather perfect.

———— ❧ ————

# *Chapter Nineteen*

*F*ONDNESS? REESE HAD watched as Harlow hurried to her room silently and closed the door quietly. No one had witnessed her return. It was as if it had never occurred. But it certainly had.

Unlike her, he'd not lost his virginity this night, but he could say for certain he'd never before felt the way he had when he'd lain with Harlow. He might have associated the feeling with her innocence, but he didn't think it was that as much as it was just… her.

He knew he would think back on this evening for the rest of his life and he would not think upon it with mere *fondness*.

He didn't think he'd ever felt so put out by a single word. And not even an offensive word at that. He'd never known such an inept description. The word lacked the emotion needed to encompass what had happened in his room. For he had been overwhelmed.

He fell back on the bed looking up at the canopy above his bed and remembered the sounds and touches they'd shared. The heat of her body and the smile on her lips. Those verdant eyes locked on his when she let desire claim her.

She'd made him feel passion in a way he'd never felt before. A way he'd never describe as *fondness*.

The next thing he knew he was opening his eyes into the

room filled with sunlight. Had he slept through the night? He guessed it had been fairly late when she'd left his room, but still he'd not woken with night terrors as was his way since Merrick had shot him on a filthy dock in London.

For a moment as he looked around he wondered if he'd dreamt her coming to his room the night before. But he need only to hold the pillow she'd lain on to catch the scent of her hair.

Thinking of another possible sign of what transpired the night before, he threw back the bedspread and looked down on the wrinkled, but snowy white, linens.

Harlow had been the only virgin he'd ever lain with, but he was to understand there was… evidence. He recalled the moment he'd entered her body. The look of surprise on her face. She'd clearly been a maid, but perhaps being older… He hoped whomever she wed would not expect proof of her virtue.

Thinking of her marrying someone stirred unease in his chest, just as it had the night before when she spoke of a child.

He'd always thought of marriage and children as something to be avoided. A duty. But now… perhaps he'd not allowed himself to think of marriage as anything other than something his mother was forcing upon him.

Like a lad, he'd obstinately refused simply because he was being told to do it. He'd made jests of his friends for falling into the trap. Yet he knew just by watching them with their wives that it was he they felt sympathy for.

They were happy when he was anything but.

Until last night with Harlow.

He rang for his valet so he might dress quickly, the sooner to get down to breakfast and see her again.

HARLOW HADN'T BEEN sure what to expect that morning. After a night filled with such joy and pleasure, she'd come down to the breakfast room to find the countess alone at the table. Reese nowhere to be seen.

Harlow knew the earl did not wish to marry, but he was also a gentleman who would see what they'd done the night before as a cue to ask for her hand again. She was surprised he hadn't already offered. Perhaps he understood she wished to marry someone who truly wanted to marry her. Not someone offering because of an obligation. Regardless, if the countess knew, she would demand they marry. So it was of the utmost importance the countess didn't suspect anything between them.

Harlow considered her options for a moment longer than she liked. Of course, she wouldn't do anything to force Reese's hand, even if he had already offered it before freely. She wouldn't use what happened between them to trap the earl.

They'd discussed what he would do with a wife who trapped him and she surely didn't wish to be set aside in the country while her husband took other lovers. He hadn't said he would, but he likely thought himself above such retribution, while Harlow knew well how a person wronged would do nearly anything to see the matter avenged.

Harlow was not so silly to think she would find a grand love affair, but she at least wanted the man who offered for her do so out of free will.

"Are you not hungry, Lady Harlow?" the countess asked. "Or do you find fault with the cook?" The woman frowned—something she seemed fond of doing—at her plate. "Only the Scots would serve meat with a side of…meat for a meal."

Harlow looked down at her own plate which contained bacon and ham as it had every morning and smiled.

"It isn't even a different meat. Ham and bacon." The woman rolled her eyes. "They are nearly the same thing. I thought the country to be filled to bulging with sheep last I visited, but it appears there is no shortage of swine. I shouldn't be surprised."

"You do not care for Scotland, my lady?" Harlow asked only to make conversation. Reese had mentioned a few times how seldom his mother came to Scotland.

"My son didn't lament on my shortcomings as a mother for refusing to visit this cold, damp place of my own accord?"

"He mentioned you haven't been here in some time but that you were happy to have been invited."

The countess *hmphed* as well as any Scot Harlow had met so far.

Harlow wasn't sure which part of her statement the woman disagreed with. Likely that she had not been invited, but ordered, to come.

"Does the earl sleep so late frequently?" the countess changed the topic so quickly Harlow blinked before answering.

"No. He's usually down before I arrive, and I'm an early riser. Belle needs to go out and since she stays in my room I get up to let her out."

"I see. I thought I heard someone wandering about at an ungodly hour. I didn't note the time."

Harlow swallowed a bit of ham and nearly choked. Had the woman heard Harlow returning to her room after she'd spend a large part of the evening in bed with the woman's son?

The room suddenly took on the temperature of the sun as Harlow took a sip of ale to clear her throat.

"I didn't hear anything."

Harlow spent much of the meal worrying Reese had fled the castle to get away from her and what they had done.

She was relieved when Mrs. Garrison slipped into the room and gave a nod to the countess, assuring her the earl was still abed sleeping soundly.

Apparently Harlow hadn't been the only one worried over the earl that morning, though for a vastly different reason.

With her worries cast aside, the woman moved on to other topics. She asked if Harlow was good with needlepoint and Harlow was able to assure her she was. Though she didn't care for it, or sitting still in general, Harlow's mother had made sure her only daughter was taught such tasks.

"Do you play an instrument?"

"Yes. The pianoforte is my favorite, but I also play the harp."

"Hmm. Good. What about dancing?"

"Of course."

"How is your French?"

"*Très bien, madame,*" Harlow answered before adding, "*e così è il mio Italiano.*" Assuring the woman that her Italian was also adequate.

"Remind me, how many siblings do you have?"

"Five older brothers. I am the youngest."

The woman fairly purred with satisfaction as she looked over Harlow, most likely trying to determine if Harlow had the fortitude to bear five sons before a daughter as is apparently the desired number of children.

"Do you ride?"

"Yes. And hunt." Which did little to impress the countess. Harlow also knew how to climb a tree and many other things that would not be considered ladylike, so she kept them to herself.

"Flower arranging?"

"Some. We have an orangery at our home in Lancashire, and grow some lovely blooms over the winter months. Nothing like the gardens here, which are exquisite."

The woman frowned and Harlow guessed her error was in enjoying Scotland more than was acceptable.

"Why do you dislike Scotland?" Harlow asked.

"In truth, I've not seen much of it. What I don't care for is this estate for after I was wed, I spent years here away from everything civilized."

Harlow swallowed down the laughter that rose from the woman's dramatics. She found the castle quite civilized indeed. It boasted an impressive library filled with all topics of books from science and the complete Stonecliff collection to gothic novels and art. The house wasn't decorated in the height of fashion, nor was it many years outdated. Though she guessed that was more

Mrs. Garrison's doing than the earl's.

The stables were modernized, and the steps that traversed the cliff to the shore were quite an undertaking.

In fact, Harlow hadn't thought of anything she missed from town. With the exception of her parents, and possibly even her brothers, Luke and Thomas, more than the other three.

"Why have you not married?" the woman asked.

Harlow thought perhaps she had brought the intrusive question about herself after asking about the woman's dislike of Scotland. Since turnabout was fair play, she decided to answer after casting a glance at the door, hoping Reese would choose that moment to enter and put an end to this uncomfortable discussion. Where was he?

"I did have offers," she started.

"I know. Twenty-four offers rejected your first Season." The woman shook her head and Harlow repressed the desire to defend herself.

"If you know that, then you must also be aware of the size of my dowry."

"I believe everyone in the King's realm is aware of the size of your dowry. Disgustingly excessive as it is." But then she tilted her head to the side as if she had figured it out on her own. "You don't wish to marry someone who only wants your money."

"Correct. As you so elegantly put it, the amount of money a man would get for taking my hand in marriage is disgustingly excessive. And it has lured many men to our drawing room clutching tight to their proffered posies and a hope that I will put their finances to rights."

"Is it true you've had proposals by mail from America?"

Harlow was not aware anyone knew of such things, but then the countess had said she knew her mother.

"Yes. But that is not counted in with the two-dozen other offers I refused." Harlow sighed. "I hope you do not think me conceited. In fact, I've recently wondered if maybe some of the men may have had a sincere interest in me, while I disregarded all of them. I don't expect love, but I don't wish to be used simply for money and my ability to produce an heir. It may seem silly, but I'd at least like to enjoy spending time with my husband."

The woman looked as if she didn't plan to answer, but eventually after a few moments of silence she relented with a nod.

"I told your mother to do something about the size of the dowry for it would only attract the worst of the ton, but she said your father refused to lower the amount because he wanted to ensure you were comfortable."

"Money doesn't make one comfortable. What am I do to with money on a chilly night?" Harlow worried the woman thought her terribly immature. She knew money was important. She wasn't a naïve girl who didn't understand that all her worldly comforts had been acquired with money. It was just that she knew a person had other needs that money couldn't satisfy.

"What of my son?"

Harlow nearly gasped. Did she know Reese was keeping Harlow plenty warm of late?

"Excuse me?" Harlow choked.

"You said he proposed to you."

Harlow wasn't sure what she should say. When she waited too long to speak, the other woman continued.

"I would assume, given the circumstances of how you came to be here, that my son—honorable as he is—offered a *sincere* proposal, not just a way to save you from any possible scandal?"

"Oh. I'm sure he was sincere." Or would have been if Harlow had only given him a chance to speak. But no, she'd cut in too soon not giving him any real consideration. If only she could go back to that moment and make a different choice.

"But you rejected his sincere offer?"

"I wouldn't say it like that. It wasn't a rejection as much as releasing him from a duty he felt honor-bound to offer."

"I think it would be a smart match." She sighed and looked out the window while once again Harlow looked at the door as if to conjure Reese. It didn't work.

One thing that was not so bad was the pleasure of knowing this formidable woman thought Harlow appropriate for her only child, but then she recalled the great lengths the countess had gone to in order to see the earl married. To anyone. She didn't seem to be very selective.

It was not so much a matter of Harlow being a good match for her son, but that she was of suitable breeding and unmarried. Still, Harlow couldn't argue that she and Reese had already formed the type of connection she had wanted with a husband.

When she heard the heavy footsteps coming closer to the room, she turned toward the door in expectation. Finally, he had come to save her.

✦ ❦ ✦

# Chapter Twenty

WHEN REESE CAME downstairs, Belle rushed up, pressing her huge head against his leg for a quick pat before she slinked into the breakfast room ahead of him, likely on the scout for some dropped morsel of food. But before he entered, someone stopped him.

"There ye be," Mrs. Garrison said as she entered behind him. "I had Rupert check in on you a few hours ago, worried you'd fallen ill."

Reese's valet had not mentioned sneaking into his room earlier when he'd helped him dress.

"I'm well," he assured her with a jaunty bow. In fact, he was more than just *well*. It seemed there was another inept word to add to his list.

"I can see that. You must have missed your mama something terrible, but you seem happy that she's here." Mrs. Garrison patted Reese's arm the way she had when he was a lad.

Reese wanted to laugh at such a misunderstanding in regards to his happiness. Of course, it was best to let the housekeeper continue on in that line of thinking for he'd not be able to explain what had really put the smile on his face.

Clearing his throat, he nodded toward the door.

"Are they both waiting?"

"Aye. Lady Harlow was feeling better this morning." She frowned and lowered her voice. "Your mother was up at dawn. Writing to let everyone in London know she's arrived in the Devil's Kingdom unscathed."

Reese chuckled at the joke. All of the staff knew Lady Breckenridge was not in Slains Castle by her own doing. His mother had made it clear what she thought of the castle and Scotland in general.

"You should get in there. Poor Lady Harlow was being interrogated about her dowry."

Reese winced and with a nod, left the housekeeper to assist the woman who'd shared his bed the night before.

When Reese entered the room, they were both looking at him. His mother with a raised brow to show she was not amused that he was late, while Lo looked desperate for him to save her. He wondered if she'd been as frighted on the Zephyr as she was now alone in this room with his mother and guessed it was likely a close thing.

He looked between them for a moment before narrowing his eyes.

"Whatever are the two of you up to?"

"Nothi—" Harlow started to speak, but the countess cut her off with, "I was just telling Lady Harlow how the two of you would make a splendid match."

"Need I remind you, mother, I brought you here to keep us from being forced into a marriage neither of us wants, not to push for something that will never happen."

He glanced at Harlow expecting to see her relief that he'd taken care of his mother's meddling, but instead she looked as if she were in a great deal of pain. From the way her hand was reached up, it seemed the pain was somewhere in the region of her chest.

Reese hadn't meant to lash out so abruptly, but his mother drove him near to madness with her constant meddling. Harlow still looked rather startled by his outburst, while his mother only frowned and looked away toward the window as if she were completely bored and totally disappointed in him.

She'd done the same ever since he'd been a lad.

He'd been so happy when he'd come down, but his mother had already put him in a foul mood. And to make it even worse, it had started to rain. Which meant he wouldn't be able to steal Harlow away to the gardens or the beach alone where he might ravish her yet again.

If that was what she'd wanted. Part of him worried what she might be thinking in the light of day. And because of his mother he wouldn't be able to just ask her how she felt about things this morning.

Why the devil had he made the countess come here?

Of course, he knew and as soon as his body calmed, he'd be glad for her presence once again, for it would mean no questions as to Lady Harlow's reputation. Even though he'd destroyed it last night.

The ton, however, would never know of such things. That's all that mattered. Appearances.

The way he appeared to be dead set against any thought of marriage to Harlow, when it had been on his mind as he'd come down the stairs only minutes earlier.

His mother did this to him. He would likely try to find a way to stop breathing if his mother told him to breathe.

"I must take Belle for a walk."

"But it's pouring and you haven't even eaten," his mother said.

He stalked to the plate that had been served the moment he walked into the room and snatched up the bacon before whipping out of the room toward the beach.

Belle whined at the top of the steps and looked back toward the house.

"Aye, lass. I will miss her this morning as well." He tucked his hat firmly on his head before descending. His dog—likely torn between duties to him and Harlow—paused twice on the way down. Both times looking back as if expecting Harlow to be there. He knew she wasn't because both times Belle stopped to look, he did as well.

"Come!" he ordered and the dog followed along. On the beach, all duty was forgotten as the dog darted up the beach sniffing around each boulder. She stopped and barked incessantly.

"Please don't let it be another woman. I'm up to my ears in them already," he muttered more to himself as he hurried to catch up with the dog who had cornered a small crab that seemed set on defending itself and its place on the beach.

"Leave it," Reese said, and then repeated when the dog hesitated and barked at the poor crustacean snapping its claws at Belle. Eventually Belle gave up to run away again, finding another creature to explore. Each time Reese called her away before she did something regrettable.

He and the dog were both soaked to the bone when they returned to the castle. Mrs. Garrison saw to sending Belle out to the stables until she was dried while Rupert had a warm bath and dry clothes waiting for him.

"Where is Lady Harlow?" he asked his valet as he slid into the warm water.

"Shall I ask Finch?"

"Aye." Reese hoped she was in a room of the house without his mother so he might go speak with her, but when the valet returned with a wince, Reese knew it wasn't to be.

"The ladies are set up in the drawing room with their needlepoint, my lord."

He'd not join them there.

As he took his seat in his study to focus on his ledgers, he considered the situation and thought perhaps it was better this way. His mother would force him to keep his distance from both ladies, and it would give him time alone to think about something other than Harlow. But an hour later he realized he hadn't done much besides think of her.

AFTER SPENDING EVERY minute of the day with Lady Breckenridge, Harlow had been looking forward to seeing Reese at dinner that evening. When the meal was served before he arrived, she realized he was still hiding.

What she wasn't sure of was if the man was avoiding her or his mother.

Perhaps he regretted what they'd done together the night before and was using his mother as an excuse to evade Harlow and any messiness he perceived between them.

Or, he really was that put out with his mother's meddling. Harlow wished she could tell the woman that her mention of them being a good match did little to help her. In fact, Harlow wondered if the man wouldn't be all the more obstinate about marriage after his mother pointed out how well they suited.

Perhaps Harlow should get the woman to protest *against* a match between them and that might make him want to marry. But again, Harlow didn't wish for a match in that way. She didn't want to look back and know that her husband had only chosen her because she'd schemed and tricked him into it.

If she couldn't have a husband who chose her for herself rather than her fortune, at least she could refrain from deception.

After dinner, Harlow played for the countess and received a nod of approval. Harlow thought that might be the most that could be expected of the woman and tried not to be deterred by the woman's lack of enthusiasm.

"Does he often take his meals in his room?" the countess asked.

Harlow opened her mouth to assure the woman he didn't, but then realized how that might sound. While it didn't prove anything, it heartened Harlow to know that he hadn't taken to his rooms until after his mother arrived.

It was coincidence that it was the same time they'd spent the night together. Still, Harlow chose to pretend it was the countess rather than her. It made her feel better.

Instead of spending the rest of the evening cozied up on the settee in the library listening to Reese read from the Stonecliff novel, she was trapped in the drawing room with the countess who had taken up her needlepoint again.

Harlow rubbed her sore finger. If she was forced to stitch anything again this evening she might run out in the rainy evening screaming.

There was a saying her father used often when he lectured her and her brothers after they'd done something ill-advised. "Be careful what you wish for." It would have suited now for instead of needlepoint, the woman had poured them each a glass of madeira and begun recounting all the suitors Harlow had rejected.

Surely she couldn't remember them all, for Harlow herself did not.

"What fault did you find in Lord Wilder?"

"Lord Wilder?" Harlow attempted to swallow. Despite the wine her throat seemed so dry. She didn't recall Lord Wilder.

"The Marquess of Kent's oldest son," Lady Breckenridge reminded her.

"Oh, yes." Harlow fought to remember anything about the man, but all she could grasp was the reason her brothers provided. And, of course, it was improper. Still, Harlow did her best. "I was told Lord Wilder looked more like the Kent's footman than Lord Kent."

Lady Breckenridge's eyes went wide. "Lady Kent had an affair with her footman?"

Harlow frowned for she wasn't sure if her brothers told her that because it was true or simply because it was an expedient way to scare her away from the gentleman. She wouldn't put it past them to fabricate a scandal where none existed.

"Well... who can really say?"

The countess laughed, or as close to a laugh as someone as

rigid as Lady Breckenridge would likely get.

"That explains a great deal about Lord Wilder."

Harlow feigned a yawn. "Please excuse me. I grow tired earlier than before. Mrs. Garrison says it's a sign I'm healing."

"Then you should retire to bed. You don't need to wait up with me. I assure you I am used to being alone." The woman waved a hand toward the door. If Harlow were a better person, she would have stayed so the woman would need not be alone this night, but Harlow had somewhere else she wished to be.

In her room, she changed into her night rail, wishing for something prettier than the plain white garment he'd purchased for her when he was being courteous.

She went to the door and stopped still. Having grown up the youngest of six children she was usually better about seeing through a plan. But it wasn't until that moment that she realized she couldn't leave her room to go to Reese's until after she was certain the countess had gone to her room for the night.

There would be nothing she could say after convincing the woman she was exhausted if Harlow was caught wandering about the corridor when Lady Breckenridge came upstairs.

Sitting with her back to the door listening for the woman's footsteps to pass her bedchamber, Harlow waited for her chance to steal away to Reese's bed again tonight.

# Chapter Twenty-One

REESE PACED HIS room long after Rupert had helped him dress for bed. His avoidance of the ladies had left him at a disadvantage. He didn't know if she might return to his room tonight. Had he been able to steal a moment alone with her, he might have been able to encourage such a rendezvous if she'd been amicable.

After an hour of waiting, he wasn't sure if the light tap at the door was real or if his anticipation had conjured up the sound, but he nearly ran the few steps to the door and opened it.

She was there.

Pulling Harlow inside, he only gave a moment of hesitation before his lips crashed down on hers. If she did not want him, she wouldn't have come to his room. And she wouldn't have looked up at him with longing in her green eyes.

If he needed any more assurance, she would definitely not be grasping tightly to his hair while her tongue explored his mouth in equal measure to the way he was exploring hers.

Then she moaned and he needed no further proof for she wanted him every bit as much as he wanted her. He was not quite so gentle as he'd been the night before. She was only one day out of being a maiden and might yet be sore, which meant he would be careful when they joined, but leading up to that point, *slow* was beyond him. He'd spent the entire day wanting her and not being able to speak to her the way he wanted. He wasn't able to make her laugh or hear her stories. He pulled her shift off and moved her to the bed with haste and hunger.

She shoved at his clothes as if they offered some offence for simply being there. When they were naked, she looked down at his body when the night before she'd only looked at him.

Her hands lightly traced the line of hair of his lower abdomen so close to where he needed attention, but her fingers moved back up over his stomach to his chest and then across one nipple causing him to suck in a quick breath. Her gaze went to his face.

"Did that hurt?"

"Only in the way that great pleasure is almost unbearable before one gives into it."

She smiled, seeming proud of herself for bringing him pleasure by her touch.

He kissed her again inadvertently trapping her hands between them. She freed them to wrap her arms low around his waist, her gentle touch moving up his back and then down. On her third circuit, she didn't stop at his waist, she went lower to his arse and squeezed him while pressing her body against his.

That was the end of his thorough examination of her neck and jaw. He moved above her and looked down to see her dark hair reaching out across his pillow like seaweed on the beach. He'd once thought her a siren and she looked like she could be one still.

"Are ye sore from last night?" he asked and she shook her head quickly.

"Is this what ye want?" he asked when his body was lined up with hers.

She nodded and pressed up again from the mattress as if hoping to make the connection herself. Her impatience cleared his concerns and he slowly pushed his way inside her body.

She moaned in the way of pleasure rather than pain and he surely made his own sound. Joining with her this night was better even than the night before. Because all of the business of virtue and discomfort was gone. They were not doing anything this night that was so resolute or changing. This was simply good.

He knew somehow that if he had a thousand nights with her they would all be better than the one before. Just because it was Harlow.

He looked down to see her gaze on him and he smiled at her. Through the lust, she managed to smile back at him. His body was near to boiling with desire, but that simple exchange cracked his heart wide open.

He didn't just want her in his bed. He wanted her in his life. When she pushed up against him again, he decided he would figure out how he could make her his sometime later. For now, he focused on her pleasure.

HARLOW HAD EXPECTED it to hurt again. Maybe not as bad as the night before for she was no longer a virgin. But after inspecting his body more thoroughly this evening, she still didn't understand how all of that had fit inside her.

But tonight there was no pain at all. Save for a small amount of soreness in her legs she'd not mentioned. She didn't think that was what he was asking about.

When he'd slid inside her that first time, she felt as if she'd been waiting a lifetime to have him inside her again. She'd heard of blue ruin and the way men and women gave up their lives to drink, unable to do anything else. She wondered now if there was a similar affliction for this. For she could see herself giving up many things to feel this way.

Certainly she'd be willing to give up hours of needlepoint with the countess. She'd forgotten she was put out with the earl for leaving her with Lady Breckenridge all day. It seemed the moment he kissed her all of her ire burned away like the morning mist.

Reese did not seem to be as careful with her this evening. It wasn't as if he was rude or reckless, he definitely saw to her satisfaction, but his thrusts were harder, his movements quicker. As if he were chasing something. Perhaps the same thing she pursued.

She began to feel that warmth growing as it had the night before. She couldn't believe it had frightened her that first time. As if she'd not survive. Now she knew how good it would be when it finally arrived.

As if Reese heard her thoughts, he reached between them pressing against the very place that spurred the feeling. She broke around him and he pounded her relentlessly until he pulled from her and shot warm fluid all over her stomach.

When he collapsed on top of her, she stared up at the canopy while running her fingers through his damp hair. She needed this in her life. She needed this man in her life. But he'd made it quite clear today that he did not.

"Should I not have come to your room this evening?" she asked.

"Oh, you definitely should not have, but I'm very glad you did." He raised his head and smiled. Maybe so she'd know how much he enjoyed what they'd done. "I was pacing the room wondering if I should have asked you or if I should go to you…"

"Had you spoken to me today we might have made arrangements." She smacked him lightly on the shoulder. "Which reminds me, I'm cross with you for leaving me all day with your mother."

"I'm sorry, lass. It seems the only thing the woman can speak of when I'm in the room is marriage and I can't take it."

She sighed. He wasn't wrong.

"She speaks to me of marriage as well."

"Aye. I'm sorry about that too. I thought I'd gotten over some of the anger, but seeing her, having her push her demands… The resentment surged."

"She is a mother who wants what is best for her child. Just like many mothers. She just goes about it much more aggressively. She doesn't seem to realize she only drives you further from doing what she wants when she pushes you as she does."

"You have the right of it. If she told me the sky was blue, I would argue it was green simply to disagree with her."

As she'd guessed. Harlow chuckled. "Both of you are so stubborn."

"This is not the time to tell me I'm like my mother," he warned with a cocked brow.

"I wouldn't think of it." She snuggled closer to him and he wrapped his arms tight around her. She loved the way he held her and didn't want him to ever let her go. But she would need to return to her room before they risked falling asleep and being found together in the morning. "I should return to my bedchamber."

He let out a sigh and squeezed her closer still.

"I don't wish for you to leave," he admitted.

She didn't want to leave him either, but she could feel sleep pulling at her. Perhaps it was penance for having lied about being tired earlier with the countess.

In truth, Harlow wished he could hold her all night. Wake her with kisses in the early hours of dawn and make love to her when they were warm and drowsy before falling asleep for another hour or two. But it was too risky.

Unless she was his wife…

He kissed her temple and then her hair before she rolled away and stood to dress. She wasn't his wife and since he was adamant about not taking a wife any time soon, she wouldn't ever be.

He helped her dress, or rather kissed along her shoulder keeping her from pulling her gown up which was the opposite of help. She chuckled as she pulled the shift up once again only to have him pull it down for a third time.

She raised up on her toes to kiss his lips and then pulled back only far enough to look into his eyes. His dark eyes seemed to look deep into her soul. Could he see what she'd been thinking? Could he know how much she wished he'd ask her to wed him for real? She'd not known at that time how very much she would come to want him.

She knew he'd only asked for the sake of propriety, but she wanted him to ask now for a different reason entirely. But he didn't.

He saw her to his door and stood watch as she rushed down the corridor, glad for the thick rug that hid her footsteps. When she paused in front of her door she looked back and gave a small wave before stealing inside and closing the door with the smallest of clicks.

Her bed chamber felt cold despite the warm night. The chill was not due to the weather but that she missed the heat of his body next to hers.

Reese would not propose again for he knew she didn't want a marriage of obligation any more than he did. But Harlow didn't want to spend her nights alone when her time at Slains Castle was over. She would set her sights on finding a husband. Someone kind and funny. Someone handsome and striking.

Someone just like Reese.

REESE RETURNED TO his bed, allowing his hand to wander over the spot of warmth where Harlow had lain moments before, and wished she was his.

Nay, not just his, but his wife.

As he'd told Harlow, he'd argue against anything his mother said or wanted because he was still angry with her, but in this, he thought he wouldn't mind so much to give her what she wanted.

Not when it was something he wanted as well.

But was it something Harlow wanted? He wasn't sure and he didn't want to risk asking to have her turn him down yet again.

As if it wasn't enough for thoughts of her to haunt his every waking minute, she also followed him in his dreams. As he slept, he was able to repeat all the things he'd done with her hours before.

She taunted him with her teasing laughter and seductive smiles. He could feel the softness of her skin and smell her sweet scent. He never wanted to wake, for in this state he never needed to worry she would leave him.

But as if his subconscious realized his darkest fear, she stepped away from him. One step and then another.

"Wait," he begged. "Don't go."

"I'm to marry," she said and then she turned her back on him and faded away.

He woke in a panic, reaching out for her. But she wasn't there. As the dream evaporated and his mind cleared, he knew she hadn't left either. She was in her room a few doors away from where he lay. She was hopefully sleeping and having sweet dreams, unlike him.

He still had a chance, but what if she didn't want him?

He let out a sigh and covered his face with his hand. This was ridiculous. He couldn't allow himself to fall for another woman who didn't want him.

Because if he asked Harlow to marry him now, after they'd been intimate, she would assume he did so out of honor and she would say no.

And that would break him.

# Chapter Twenty-Two

HARLOW WOKE WITH a smile, despite the soreness in her muscles and other delicious places. She waited as she'd done the day before, for some feeling of regret but was met with nothing but disappointment that she would need to wait the entire day to be with him again.

One thing was for certain, she was going to marry someone soon. She couldn't imagine going back to the life of a spinster after Reese had shown her how exciting intimacy could be.

She practically floated down the stairs to the breakfast room, excited to see the man responsible for making her feel so satisfied. She only faltered slightly when she found the room in the same state as she had the day before, without the earl.

She greeted the countess with a smile and took her seat. A footman covered her lap with a napkin and set a plate before her as another footman did the same for the woman seated at the end of the table.

"Are we not going to wait for Lord Breckenridge?" she asked. She knew Reese had hidden away the day before so not to deal with his mother's schemes, but she'd thought he'd cast that plan aside so as not to abandon her.

"The earl is not in residence so we will eat without him or starve."

Harlow blinked at the woman who had taken a knife and fork to her meal.

"Is he walking Belle early this morning?" Belle had not returned to the house after Harlow had let her out earlier that morning.

"No. He's gone to Inverness on business."

"Oh, I see," Harlow said, though she did not see. She'd found the night before to be wonderful, and he was avoiding her yet again. No, even worse, he wasn't even in the castle. He'd left her here.

She wanted to think it was his mother he was evading, but why would he have gone so far away that they wouldn't even have their nights alone?

After breakfast, Harlow walked along the garden path with the dog, as the countess disliked all things outdoors. Belle slunk along beside Harlow as if she missed the man as well.

"He just left us without so much as a note or a word of goodbye." Harlow twisted her mouth to the side. "I suppose he might have said farewell to you for you would have likely been out when he left."

She wondered if speaking to a dog was a bad sign. When Belle whined, she thought maybe it wasn't so bad if the dog spoke back.

"I miss him too," she said. "When he returns, he and I must talk."

Belle's scruffy ears perked up and she launched toward the steps that went down to the ocean.

"Belle! I said *talk* not walk." But that only hurried Belle along faster. Soon she was gone down the stairs. Harlow stood at the top looking down at the stone steps leading down to the beach. They were still damp from yesterday's rain. Harlow had never traversed them without Reese to assist, but the earl wasn't there and if his dog got hold of something on the beach and became ill, Harlow would feel quite guilty for not braving a flight of stairs to keep it from happening.

Looking over her shoulder she took the first step and then the next. She'd turned to the side so there was more space for her foot and was going step by step. At this pace it might take all day for her to get down to the sand, but she was making progress.

When the dog began barking in earnest, Harlow winced. What creature had the dog cornered and what damage could be done? In a hurry now, she'd turned to pick up the pace, but slipped, her previously injured ankle holding firm but she was unable to gain traction. She stumbled down three steps and reached out to catch herself on the railing, but the wood couldn't hold a grown woman moving at such a rate of speed.

She found herself falling. For a moment she seemed to hang in the air, but then her body slammed against a rock and then another. She reached out, grasping for anything to stop her descent to the roaring waves and jagged rocks below.

Gripping onto a ledge, she found herself hanging and swinging in the breeze. Sparing a glance down, she regretted it instantly when she realized if she let go she would fall to her death.

Her kid gloves had provided some protection from the stone edge, but they were not made for their grip. She was slipping, and she was not strong enough to pull herself back up. Looking straight ahead toward the cliff she saw a wider ledge that housed a few nests of mud and grass.

She hoped she would not dislodge any inhabitants, but it was her only chance. With her final bit of strength, she swung over to the ledge and landed with an umph.

The shorter ledge was tilted away from the stairs, but was deep enough that she could sit or even lay down if she needed to. She hoped she wouldn't need to.

REESE URGED HIS horse faster. It was growing dark and he wanted to be home in time for supper. Not only because he was near to starving, but because he wanted to apologize to Harlow for having left her without a word.

He'd no sooner arrived in Inverness than he realized he shouldn't have come.

After his bad dreams where Harlow left him to marry another, Reese had fallen asleep again only to be haunted by Merrick. While he wasn't able to do anything about Harlow, he thought he might be able to exorcise the ghost of Merrick if he could help catch the man.

But Reese was no longer an agent, and his being seen there could very well hamper the mission for the other agents to find Merrick. So he'd left to return home.

Every mile he grew closer to home, the more he wanted to see Harlow and apologize for leaving her without a word.

Surely his mother would have something to say about him running off without word of his plans to return. He'd face her if it meant spending the night with Harlow. He'd tried once again to put distance between them only to be pulled back to her like metal filings to a magnet.

When he took the hill that gave him his first glimpse of Slains Castle, he almost thought it was aflame at first. But then he noticed it was only that light came from nearly every window.

The reflection of flames on the stone were coming from torches. At least three of them flitted about the garden.

"What the devil?" he whispered as he urged his horse into motion again.

Upon pulling up his mount in front of the castle, no one seemed to give the master of the house a bit of attention.

He waved down a young boy who worked in the stable.

"What has happened?"

"'Tis the lady, my lord. She's missing."

"Which lady?" Reese demanded. It shouldn't have mattered. Even if it were his mother, he would be concerned. Or he thought he would. If given enough time.

"The young one."

Harlow was missing? Had she left to go home? Perhaps in light of staying there with only his mother for company she'd given up on her quest for vengeance and returned to London. But she would have needed funds. And a carriage.

"Are any of the horses or carriages missing?" he asked the lad who was taking his horse away.

"Nay, my lord. All's accounted for 'sept this gent. And now he's home too."

It didn't mean Harlow didn't leave, but if she had, she'd gone under her own power so she couldn't have gone far.

Rather than speak to the lad about the situation, Reese made for the stairs. He found the inside of the castle as active as outside. He spotted someone who might be able to share the details.

"Finch."

"Oh, my lord. I'm that glad ye've returned. Lady Harlow is missing. Last anyone saw her was this morning after breakfast. She went out to the gardens with Belle and didn't return."

"And Belle?" he asked because if the dog was missing as well, at least he knew Harlow wasn't completely unprotected.

"She showed up alone by the kitchen door this afternoon." The man pointed toward his study where Belle liked to nap. "She's fine, but I wish she could talk for she might have seen something."

Reese nodded.

"We only noticed Lady Harlow wasn't in the house when she didn't come down for supper. A maid took a tray up to her as we figured she'd be hungry for missing the noon meal. But she wasn't in her room."

"My mother?"

"She's in the solar. She's not seen the lass since this morning."

Reese hurried toward the solar to find his mother sitting by the window with her needlepoint in hand, though she wasn't actively working on it.

"What did you do?" he accused when she turned to him.

"Me? Why would you think I did anything to the lass?"

"I don't think ye did anything to her. But did ye say something to make her want to flee Slains? If you were pestering the woman about marriage again, I'll put you out on your ear."

"It is nice to see how much trust and love you have for me, Son." She rolled her eyes.

Reese had no patience for sarcasm or dramatics.

"Mother."

"I didn't say anything. We spoke at breakfast, and I don't even recall what the topic was. Just pleasantries. Nothing about marriage."

Reese didn't know if he believed that for it seemed to be the only thing the woman could talk about of late. Still, he didn't think Harlow would leave because his mother pressured her about marriage. Lo was made of sterner stuff than that.

She wouldn't be reckless enough to set off on foot, no matter how mad she may have been. Which meant she didn't leave.

"If she didn't leave, she is still on the grounds."

"Unless someone took her," his mother mentioned with genuine worry.

Reese wasn't one for mathematics but even he knew the odds of Harlow being kidnapped twice in shy of two months was unlikely. Merrick didn't know she was at his home. He probably thought her dead. Which means he wouldn't have come looking for her.

Reese would start with the most rational place she could be. In the garden. As he descended the stairs, his stomach twisted with worry. The fact that Harlow hadn't returned to the house by now meant she wasn't able to. Which meant she was injured, or…

He shook his head. He'd not allow that thought to take root. He was going to find her and she would be fine. She had to be.

Yet even as he headed down the main corridor, he knew it was not a good sign that Belle had returned alone.

Stopping in the study he saw the dog lying in front of the unlit hearth. As if waiting for him. Her head picked up when he entered the room.

"She's been worrying by the door, but every time we leave her out she runs for the steps to the beach and then comes right back." Finch shrugged.

Reese cocked his head, knowing his dog was bright and knew not to go down to the beach without him.

"Was Belle wet when she showed up at the kitchen?" Reese asked the butler, having had an idea.

"Aye. I guess she was. She must have been down..." He turned to Reese with wide eyes. "Ye don't think the lass went down to the beach by herself, do you? We've not checked there. She's never gone down there without you."

Reese cut through the drawing room to the terrace. He crossed the lawn to the stone steps that led down to the beach. It was too dark now to see down to the shore but he knew the tide would be coming in. He recalled seeing her lying on the sand with the waves crashing around her legs and worried he'd find her in the same state as before. Or worse.

Taking a lantern from Finch, he started carefully down the steps. He paused at the third landing where the stairs turned, for the banister was missing.

His heart nearly came out of his throat to see the splintered wood. If she'd fallen from here she would have surely landed on the large boulders strewn across that part of the beach.

"Oh, dear," Finch said.

"Harlow!" Reese shouted. His stomach twisted when the only answer to his call was the sound of the waves crashing against the shore. He set the lantern down so he could cup his hands around his mouth and yelled again. "Harlow!"

He tilted his head, listening. He thought he heard her voice, but wasn't sure if in his worry, he'd imagined it.

He went down another flight of stairs and called, "Harlow!"

*Please answer*, he begged. But there was no response.

# Chapter Twenty-Three

HARLOW HEARD HER name again and shouted with all her might to answer. Unfortunately, she'd lost her voice earlier in the day when she'd been calling for help in vain. And now when she needed it the most, she could barely rasp a response.

And then she saw the light from a lantern. Turned as she was, she could barely make out Reese in the glow. He'd come home.

As the sun had retreated with the approaching evening, Harlow began to worry she'd have to spend the night out there on her small perch. And now he was there, but he couldn't see her and she couldn't call out to him with any volume.

She picked up a piece of stone from her hidden crevice and while clutching the wall, she hurled a rock about the size of a peach pit toward the man.

She heard it clunk against the step, but couldn't be sure if he'd seen it. She quickly picked up another and another. Fortunately this ledge was filled with shards of rock. She could keep throwing them at him.

"Harlow? Might you stop hurling rocks at me so we might rescue you?" Reese asked. Harlow slumped against the wall and broke into tears. She'd not cried the whole day despite having no idea how long she might be there before someone found her, but now with a rescue imminent, she couldn't stop shaking and crying.

"Go get all the rope from the stables," Reese ordered someone and she saw one of the lights went off up the stairs. "Are you injured?" he asked.

"No," she croaked as loud as she could, but he must not have heard over the roar of the ocean below.

"Harlow? Can you answer?"

She closed her eyes in frustration and more tears fell. She cast them aside with a brush of her hand and picked up a rock. Instead of throwing it at him, she tapped it against the sides of her enclosure.

Three loud smacks of the stone.

"I hear you, but you must not be able to speak."

She again knocked along the wall three steady beats.

"Three means yes, and one means no. Are you injured?"

She responded with one.

"Good. That's good. We're going to get you. Don't move."

As if she had the option of moving. Since darkness had fallen, she didn't even want to shuffle about in her safe area for she could no longer see the edge.

She heard a number of people descending the steps, the murmuring of voices.

"Finch said you've found her," Mrs. Garrison asked.

"Aye. It seems she fell through the rail and is on a cliff ledge. Please go have blankets and a hot meal prepared, Mrs. Garrison. Are you hungry, Harlow?" he called to her.

She tapped the rock three times, though she wished should could have responded verbally. She would have told him she was famished.

"Why can she not answer?" Mrs. Garrison asked.

"I'm not sure, but she's able to communicate. Let's get her off the rocks and we'll go from there. The rest of you stay back. And watch the railing. It needs to be repaired."

A few minutes longer and she heard more shuffling, then Reese's voice came to her in the darkness.

"Harlow, we'll be tossing over a rope with a stick tied to it. I can't see where you are in the dark, but if you can cover your face so I don't hit you. Don't reach for the rope; let it come to you. I don't want to risk your falling."

She didn't want that either for she knew if she fell from this place there was nothing to catch her fall.

She knocked her rock three times to indicate that yes, she understood.

She heard a stick clatter along the rock, but it didn't reach the opening.

"Did that reach you?" he yelled.

She tapped the rock once.

"Was it too far or too short?"

She didn't know how to answer with rock signals.

"Uh, two taps for too short. Four taps for too far. Followed by a pause and then two taps for too high and four taps for too low."

She tapped twice to tell him it was too short, but she hadn't noticed the height so she didn't tap again after the pause.

"I'm throwing again. The same height but farther."

It took six more tries, with her signaling between each attempt before the stick came to rest at her foot and she was able to step on it. Very carefully she reached down and picked it up. She gave it a slight tug.

"You have hold of it?"

She tapped three times.

"Tie it snuggly around your waist. Do you know a good knot so you'll not be pulled loose?"

She knocked three times. She'd learned many knots from her brothers. Mostly when they used them to tie her up when she was captured during one of their games.

"Tap the stone five times when you are secure and ready to be pulled over."

She tucked the stone under her arm as she tied a knot before tying a second and a third knot for safe measure.

She heard shuffling and talking but didn't know what they said for she was so focused on the knotting of the rope. She gave it a few firm tugs and then tapped with her rock five times.

When the earl spoke this time, he was higher above her.

He instructed her to knock twice when all the slack was out of the rope and she could feel them pulling. She did as she was told.

"You should be able to step out and put your feet against the rock. We'll pull you up, but use your feet to walk up so you are not dragged against the stone. Do you understand?"

She knocked three times.

Then she paused and took a deep breath. She would need to trust Reese enough to step out into the darkness. She didn't hesitate more than a few seconds for she trusted Reese.

"I've got you, Harlow. I'll not let anything happen to you. I promise."

With that she stepped out and hoped for the best.

REESE FELT THE weight of her on the rope and ordered the groom to move the horse forward very slowly. It went against every instinct he had for he only wanted Harlow in his arms. To know she was safe.

But he couldn't rush. To do so could cause injury to the woman he realized he cared for more than himself. Which was something he needed to keep to himself. For if his staff saw him grab hold of Harlow and kiss her silly, they would be forced before the minister by morning.

"Go slowly, Harlow," he said when it seemed she was pulling at the rope frantically.

Soon he saw movement within the range of his lantern light. Her hair was as dark as the night so it was her face he saw first, and he gasped with the pain in his chest. His throat burned with emotion he needed to keep hidden. When she was close enough for him to let go of the rope to grab her, he did. Pulling her against his chest. He would tell everyone it was necessary for her safety, but he couldn't take another breath without feeling her against him warm and alive.

"Hold!" he called. "I have her. Unhook the rope from the horse."

He tugged at the knot around her waist and when she was free turned to make sure no one was looking before he pulled her close again, kissing her lips and her face and her neck until the light from above moved closer.

Having to pull away from her was the hardest thing he'd ever had to do. Only knowing that he'd have the opportunity to hold her soon when they were alone in his room allowed him to loosen his grip.

"Are you all right?" he asked again.

"Yes. Thank you," she said in a light, raspy voice. "I lost my voice from screaming. But no one heard."

"I'm so sorry I wasn't here. I should have been here. This is my fault," he whispered.

His staff descended upon her, helping her up the stairs, wrapping her in blankets. Even his dog barked her welcome and ran around in circles, obviously happy with her return.

She was shuffled away from him to be taken care of. Inside the house she was fed and fussed over. Belle refused to leave her side and Reese saw just how much everyone loved her.

Perhaps even himself. In a very different way.

His mother joined the gathering and brushed Harlow's dark hair over her shoulder.

"I'm glad you are all right. I was so worried," his mother admitted showing emotions she kept securely hidden away from everyone. Perhaps he was more like her than he'd realized.

The countess left Harlow's side to come stand by him.

"I'm not sure if it was a trick of the light or a shadow, but it looked as if the two of you were kissing when she made it up from the ledge," his mother said without looking at him. Her casual gaze was turned to watch all the hustle and bustle.

"It was most definitely a trick of the lighting. Whyever would I kiss a guest?" he lied.

"I'm not sure, perhaps for the same reason you have not been able to take your eyes off of her?"

Apparently, Reese had been hovering much like his dog.

"I don't know what you speak of. I only want to ensure my guest is unharmed. What kind of host would I be if I didn't see after her care and make certain she didn't need a doctor?"

His mother chuckled. He froze and turned toward the sound he so rarely ever heard. His mother did not laugh often.

"Very well. I shall pretend I didn't see anything." She raised a brow. "For now."

He glared at the woman who would do almost anything to see him wed as soon as possible.

"You *didn't* see anything, mother. See that ye remember that."

She waved her hand as if she didn't care in the slightest about his unspoken threats. So long as she didn't cause any trouble or put Harlow's reputation at risk, his mother could think whatever she wished.

A few hours later he was in his room waiting by his door for her to come to him as she had the other nights. When he'd waited nearly half an hour, and she hadn't arrived, he tied the belt on his banyan and all but ran from his room. He lifted his hand to knock lightly at her door, but it opened before he could complete the knock.

She gasped when she all but ran into him.

"I was just coming to your room." Her voice was still slightly rough from her hours of screaming for help. A wave of guilt washed over him. He should have been there.

"You were late," he said, hating that he sounded accusatory. She obviously didn't realize how much he needed to hold her and feel for himself that she was whole and unharmed. He'd not be able to sleep without seeing her.

She tilted her head. "I'm sorry, I didn't realize we'd specified a time for our secret meetings in your room."

She was smiling, but he didn't find it funny. Later, he would see the humor in her comment, but at the moment he was wrought tight with concern.

"I was worried," he admitted. His feelings had come to the surface and he was having trouble burying them once again.

"I'm fine. It's only that Mrs. Garrison had stayed longer than was normal. If you'd come only a few minutes earlier you would have run into her when she was leaving."

They surely wouldn't have wanted that. Though Mrs. Garrison was far more preferable if they were caught than his mother who was likely looking to catch them.

"Do you wish to come in?" she offered and since they were standing there conspicuously in the hall, he nodded and entered the room.

He kissed her as he normally did in the evenings after wanting her all day, but for some reason this time when his lips touched hers something seemed to overwhelm him. He was nearly swept away with it.

He pulled back to look into her bright green eyes.

"I could have lost you," he whispered as if surprised to hear the thought himself.

"If I were a cat one might say I only have seven lives left. Well..." She shook her head. "Probably more like five. There were two other situations when I was younger."

"It's not funny," he said, not liking the cavalier way she was handling the fact that she might have plummeted to her death that afternoon. And yes, surviving her jump overboard was another close call, but he hadn't known her then. He hadn't cared the way he did now. With his entire being. "Good God," he said out loud without meaning to. But he was just so shocked to realize how very much he cared for her.

"You have that look you get before you avoid me for the entire day."

"I do not have a look," he argued, but she was probably right. He didn't know what to do with his feelings so he'd felt it was best to stay clear so he'd not risk telling her everything.

"Oh, but you do, my lord. I believe it's the look of surprise to realize you like me more than you planned to allow."

"Are ye a witch?" It was if she'd called the thoughts right from his head.

"No. Just observant." She frowned. "Are you going to avoid me again?"

She looked saddened by this possibility and he realized how much he had hurt her by abandoning her. Perhaps as much as he'd hurt himself. But rather than say that, he took a page from her book and made a jest.

"I can't really leave you alone, can I? Who knows what might happen to you if left to your own devices."

She smiled, seeming satisfied with his answer.

"We are together now," she said with a teasing smile. She tilted her head as she reached for the sash of her dressing gown. But he put his hands out to still hers. Of course, he wanted her. He thought if he lived to be a hundred and three he would want her nearly every day, but tonight he wanted something different.

"Not tonight," he said. When she blinked, he thought his voice might have been too harsh. "I'm not refusing you. I would like to hold you, if you're agreeable. You gave me quite a scare today and I just want to feel you in my arms, warm and breathing."

She swallowed and he saw her eyes turn glassy. It seemed she was not oblivious to the danger she'd been in, but had preferred to brush it aside rather than allow it to fester.

"I'm sorry. I don't mean to bring up things you don't wish to think about—"

She cut off his words by reaching up to wrap her arms around his neck and pull him close. He heard a few sniffles and felt the way her body shook with quiet sobs.

He held her tight and gave her as long as she needed to deal with her emotions. In fact, he would be quite happy to never have to let her go.

# Chapter Twenty-Four

A FTER A GOOD cry, Harlow felt much better. Reese was a perfect gentleman to not mention the way she'd fallen apart in his arms. He'd also not mentioned the mess she surely looked or the dampness she'd left all over his shirt.

She'd thought she was fine, but it seemed this near-death experience was one too many.

It did give her an idea though.

"I've thought of another thing I'd like to do to get back at my uncle for what he did," she told Reese.

He chuckled and drew her closer. "It was already quite devious, but tell me your plan."

For the next hour they discussed the elaborate details of how she could ensure her uncle would be begging for mercy. Reese offered his own ideas and between the two of them she felt confident it would be even more terrifying than their previous plan. The man deserved everything she had devised to torment him. And when she was done, and he was broken before her, she would be able to put all of this behind her.

At least that was what she was hoping for.

"He will rue the day he betrayed me," she said sounding a bit sinister with her rough voice and threatening demeaner. "Do you think your mother will help me with my costume?"

"The woman seems determined to stir up scandal of late, so I'm sure she would be elated to help ye with your dramatic revenge plot."

"You don't think it's too much?" she asked.

He laughed and she realized how much she liked hearing it. He didn't laugh as much as he should, she would make it her goal to have him laughing more often.

"I definitely think it's too much, but it's perfect."

When her eyes grew heavy, he kissed her softly and got out of her bed where they'd been lounging comfortably.

"I shall leave you to your rest. You had a tiring day and if I stay I'll be in danger of falling asleep here."

The idea of sleeping next to him all night, where he might banish her nightmares, was tempting. She thought of how nice it must be to wake up next to someone in the morning. All the things they could do in their room before starting the day.

It wasn't until she was snuggled down in her covers and she heard the soft click of the door that she realized they hadn't been intimate as they'd been before. He'd said he'd wanted to hold her, but she assumed he would get to those other things when he was assured she was fine.

Perhaps, she thought, lying together talking and touching was the most intimate they'd ever been. Even if their bodies hadn't joined, their hearts had. She knew he truly cared for her. And she certainly cared a great deal for him as well.

If he proposed again, she wouldn't hesitate to accept, for it was clear he didn't want her for money, or simply because he'd taken her virtue. They could be quite happy together. Especially when they could share a bed without having to sneak around.

If he asked simply because he wished to rather than because of his mother's threats and pressure she would be happy to become his wife. And until then she would be satisfied being his lover. And friend.

The next morning after dressing, she made her way to the breakfast room and smiled when she found the earl in his place at the head of the table.

"Good morning, my lord." She dipped a curtsey to Reese before turning to the countess. "Lady Breckenridge."

"Good morning," his mother greeted her while Reese simply winked and waited for her to take her seat before he dug into his meal.

"I was going to tell my mother of your plan, but thought you might want to share your diabolical scheme yourself."

As they ate, Harlow shared her thoughts. At first, the countess seemed shocked by Harlow's deviousness, but then after some thought she agreed to help. And even came up with some ideas herself.

"That is very good," Reese said. "Shall we meet after luncheon to start working on things? As for now, I am going to take Harlow and Belle on a stroll that hopefully results with the three of us returning to the house."

His mother raised her brow at Harlow. "See that you do, young lady. We'll not have you hanging about on a cliff all day."

"I wouldn't think of it," Harlow promised and got up to take his offered arm. They were quiet as they walked across the lawn to the gardens. Belle had already run off to chase a rabbit, leaving them alone. As soon as they were ensconced in the shadows of the trees, Reese turned to her and kissed her thoroughly.

"I wanted only to hold you last night, but I woke up wanting you fiercely," he admitted while kissing up her throat.

"Here?"

"Yes. I'll not make it to the evening. I need you now. No one comes out here but us. My staff is busy and my mother abhors the outdoors. We will be alone."

He kissed her again. This time his need shifted to something deeper.

Opening her eyes after his kiss she looked into his chocolate gaze and wished he would be the man who wanted her for the rest of his life. But he'd already asked—or tried to—and she'd turned him down. How was she to communicate that his offer would be better received now?

She let out a breath heavy with disappointment. She'd known the earl had only proposed that first day out of obligation. For he'd not known her at all. Definitely not enough to warrant sharing his life with her.

Maybe he wouldn't ever offer again. She'd not met a man more dead set against marriage. Even her horde of bachelor brothers did not detest the institution as ardently as Lord Breckenridge. Though she did wonder if he protested a bit too much. Could it be that the man was doing his best to convince himself it was something he didn't want because he saw it as something unattainable under the conditions he'd mentioned?

He'd said he only wanted to marry a woman who wanted him, not a title or what he could give her. And definitely not because they were forced to marry because of society's dictates. But she did not want him for material things. She genuinely liked spending time with him. Perhaps without meaning to they had inadvertently met the criteria of an agreeable match.

Interesting. And she may have thought more on it if the man had not leaned closer and kissed her again. This time instead of a single, soft press of his lips against hers he consumed her mouth, thrusting his tongue inside to spar with hers.

She didn't realize he had pulled her onto his lap until they broke for air and she realized she was pressed up against him. A place she liked extremely well, but would have enjoyed better without their clothes in the way.

"I wasn't sure if you would want this today," she said. When he'd only wanted to hold her last night, she'd wondered if he'd tired of her already, but she realized that they both needed something deeper the night before, after such a trying day.

He kissed the edge of her jaw with a smile on his lips. "I imagine I will want this every day until you shoo me away."

She was the one to lean in this time. Placing her palms against his cheeks she held him so she might kiss him as deeply as she wished. Kissing, however, didn't seem like enough.

It was absurd to think that she had only kissed him for the first time days before when now it seemed like it was her sole reason for living. Or perhaps it was what they'd done in his bed. How could she want something so intensely she'd gone years without?

The answer didn't matter for as she moaned and shifted restlessly on his lap she knew what she wanted and didn't care about the reason why or that it was too much.

She felt his cock pressing against her leg and it pushed another wave of heat and need through the core of her body.

"I need you," she said, unsure if she should have admitted to such a thing, but not caring about that either if it got her what she wanted sooner.

He looked around in a daze as if surprised to find them outside in the garden. She did the same, realizing that they would likely have to wait until that night to meet in his room and quench their desires. It seemed too long to wait.

He must have seen her need, for he reached low and slid his hand under her skirts. His warm fingers heated her skin as they slid up to the place she wanted him to touch.

When he did, he groaned.

"So wet," he said more to himself and she felt his cock lurch against her as if it were of its own mind to free itself from his breeches.

When his fingers delved into her, she gasped and settled against the exquisite invasion. "Yes."

He continued to touch her both inside and outside her body until she felt that spinning she'd felt the night before.

"Yes," she said again or maybe for the hundredth time, she couldn't be sure.

And then his thumb pressed more firmly against that spot and her body jolted and throbbed as the air left her body and didn't return for some time later.

She gasped against him as her body sagged in release, but she felt him still hard against her. When she was able to open her eyes and the world came back into focus, she slid back and reached for him, touching him through the fabric.

He grunted as if in pain and pulled her hand away.

"I just need a moment."

"A moment to finish?" she asked wondering what she might do to help him as he'd helped her.

"No. For it to go away."

"Why would you wish it to go away?"

"Because it will be some time until I can do anything to relieve it."

He had used his fingers to bring her to climax; she looked at her bare hand and thought surely she could do the same for him.

She reached for the buttons of his breeches and he took her hands into his.

"What are you doing?"

"If I were to touch you… there." She nodded to his engorged member. "Would it not feel as good as your touch felt for me?"

"It would feel wonderful, but we are in the garden and you are a lady."

She cocked her head and laughed.

"You just touched me intimately and sated my overheated body in the garden. Why would I not be able to do the same to you? Our crimes are not negated by only completing half the infraction, my lord."

She gave him what she hoped was a saucy grin and reached for his breeches again. This time he didn't stop her while she struggled with the blasted buttons that eventually gave way so she could put her hand inside to grasp him.

"Dear God, Harlow," he said as he squeezed his eyes closed. She knew she had done the right thing as she stroked him, mimicking the movements they had engaged in the night before.

Reese's breathing picked up and he held tight to her until he groaned and stilled. She felt hot liquid spill through her fingers. The same as she'd felt on her stomach the night before.

She pulled her hand free looking down at the mess and wondered what she was to do now. But after a few deep breaths, the earl reached into his jacket and pulled out a handkerchief. He cleaned her hand while looking at her instead.

"Thank you," he said.

She smiled, feeling quite powerful in having been able to bring him release on her own.

"You are quite welcome. Now that we have seen to that, should we find out who stole the art from the rook's tower?" she said mentioning the book they had yet to finish. He'd brought it out with them.

He grinned and handed over the book so she might start reading first.

# Chapter Twenty-Five

S NEAKING AROUND WITH Harlow was growing tedious and Reese wondered for the thousandth time why he'd ever written to his mother and asked her to come. For the countess was the greatest risk to Harlow's reputation.

That very morning he'd nearly given them away when he'd come into the breakfast room and caught himself just shy of bending to kiss Harlow. And only a few moments ago, his mother had entered his study when he was helping Harlow put her hair to rights after an extremely zealous round of kissing. And touching.

If they were not careful, his mother would be the reason they would be forced to marry after all. Wouldn't she just love that? Not only to see him married, but married to a friend's—make that a duchess's—daughter.

He couldn't let the woman win.

"Are you well? You seem angry," Harlow asked when she'd finished reading the last chapter.

"Apologies. I'm not angry with ye. It's just my mother. I wish I would have realized how much of an impediment she would become. Perhaps I was hasty in asking her to come."

"If I'm to understand correctly, it didn't sound like you asked her at all. She said there were orders and threats, my lord."

"My thoughts had been to protect your reputation. Had I known then how thoroughly I would end up ruining you myself, I wouldn't have bothered." He offered a smile, feeling the guilt seep all the way down to his feet. He'd wanted to protect her and now…

"It's strange that it is called ruination, don't you think?" she asked as she kissed him under the jaw. "When I feel anything but ruined. I feel free and powerful. Please don't regret anything we've done and hopefully do in the future."

"I should regret it, but I don't. Instead, I feel only guilt for having taken something so precious from you."

"You didn't take anything from me. It was freely given."

"A gift for your future husband. Not meant for me." Mixed in with the guilt was an underlying jealousy of a man neither of them yet knew. The husband she would one day have.

Harlow shrugged. I feel like it was I who received a gift. I wanted to live. Or perhaps it was that I wanted to feel alive. And you gave that to me." She chuckled. "I'm sure I'm not explaining it correctly, but I can assure you what I feel is far from ruined."

"I'm glad you are enjoying yourself, but if my mother were to catch us, she would demand we wed and neither of us wanted marriage in that way." He watched her closely to see her reaction. Had she considered it? Would she answer differently if he were to ask her again in this moment where they were sharing their souls?

He opened his mouth to ask, but the words got trapped in his throat. He'd promised himself he'd not utter the request again until he was certain of the answer he would receive. And he didn't know what she might say.

Proposing would open him up to two possible outcomes. Endless happiness, or utter destruction.

ALL THIS TALK of ruination had Harlow uneasy. After they'd shared a blissful moment in the garden, they'd gone back to their book. When it was his turn to read, she studied him closely. The way his lashes were darker then his hair as they brushed his cheeks when he blinked.

She loved the low rumble of his voice with the Scottish lilt to certain words. She could listen to him speak for hours. She watched his fingers as he turned the pages and knew how they felt when he touched her skin or even deep inside her body.

But as much as he roused her body to pleasure, he also had a way of rousing her heart to feel things she'd never felt before. She was growing more certain each day, the feeling was love.

She worried when she left Scotland she would miss him terribly and she didn't think any other man would save her from wanting Reese.

Aboard Merrick's ship she'd promised herself she would accept the next proposal of marriage she received. After the fear was gone, she'd amended that pledge somewhat. She would seriously consider marriage with a man who met her own criteria rather than that of her brothers. So long as the man was kind and his request was offered out of genuine interest, she would accept. And now she realized she only wanted to marry one man. Reese.

He'd tried to offer and she'd put him off. Now she wondered how she might encourage him to propose again.

Belle ran ahead of them as they walked back to the castle. They held hands up until they breached the trees where they could be seen by anyone in the house who cared enough to look.

The countess was likely in the drawing room which faced the grounds. And she would be looking. She seemed eager to catch them in some situation that would force their hand.

At the door Reese pulled her to the side quickly to steal a final kiss where no one could see them.

"I'll see you soon," he said as he turned for his study and she for the drawing room where she would spend the afternoon with his mother. Usually, Harlow lamented having to sit in near silence with the woman, while stabbing her fingers repeatedly in an effort to create a crude rendering of a flower. Especially when she would rather spend the day with Reese looking at real flowers in the garden while kissing.

But today she had something she wished to speak about with the countess.

Rather than launch into the topic immediately, Harlow started with easier discussion.

"It is a lovely day. I'm surprised you don't wish to sit on the terrace."

"The terrace has limited shade and I do not need to be harassed by insects."

Harlow smiled. She could argue there were few insects on the terrace and there was a cool breeze coming off the ocean that made the sun bearable if one could not avoid it entirely.

Belle rested her head on Harlow's foot as she stretched out for her midday nap.

"Does the beast have to follow you everywhere?" the woman said as her nose pinched up in distaste. "She smells."

"Should I send her away?" Harlow asked, knowing the woman would not be so rude as to make her order the dog from the room.

"No. The beast looks comfortable. I'll simply have to bear it, I guess."

Harlow pressed her lips together to hide her smile.

"Did the earl say when they would be finished with the repairs on the steps? The insidious hammering is not good for my nerves." The woman sent another look toward the glass doors where the men were working.

"I'm sure it will not be so long. I didn't make such a large hole after all."

The woman didn't crack a smile at Harlow's joke, but she stopped frowning which was an improvement at least.

"You seem unhappy here, my lady." Harlow darted a look to see the surprise on the woman's face.

"I don't think it strange that a person not enjoy being forced into something they didn't want to do."

Harlow struggled to keep her satisfaction hidden away when the woman went for the bait straightaway.

"I imagine that is to be expected. I do not fancy being told what to do either. At home I'm constantly ordered about and manipulated by my brothers. To their detriment. For once I realize what they want from me, I am usually dead set against it. No one likes being contorted to others' whims. Even earls."

The woman's dark eyes flared with interest.

"I see. It is a good point you make."

"Oh, I don't know that I made a point." Except for the one she just poked through the skin of her thumb. "I am simply making an observation."

"Do you have any other observations you wish to share?"

Harlow tilted her head to the side deciding how to broach the next topic.

"You said you know my mother."

"Yes. I don't know that I could call us dear friends, but we were presented at court at the same time so there was a certain bond. Your father and the late earl were friends."

"Do you think I am like my mother?"

The woman set her stitching aside to take a long look at Harlow. "You certainly look like her. Though I'd never known your mother to be so prone to life threatening events."

"You're right. My mother is rather calm, while I grow restless when I sit too long."

The countess nodded. "You get that from your father. A trait he seems to have passed on to all of his children for your brothers are full of energy as well."

"I do think it normal for children to get parts of their personalities from both parents, do you agree?"

"Yes. I think that is the way of heredity." She tilted her head seeming quite curious.

"It's just that while my personality more closely resembles

that of my father, I am more comfortable with my mother. We don't always get on with people who are too similar to us."

Her brow rose when she realized where this conversation was going.

"Another good observation, Lady Harlow. You are wise beyond your years. What a wonderful daughter-in-law you will make to a lucky woman when you marry her son."

It seemed Harlow was not the only one directing the conversation strategically. She would not let the opportunity pass.

"I do hope so. Of course, I don't know how well received it would be if I were to tell a potential mother-in-law that she should not push for a match so earnestly for she was causing more harm than good."

The woman smiled then, something more terrifying than when she glared or sneered.

"I'm certain if the woman was smart she would receive the information very well, indeed."

"One can only hope," Harlow concluded, knowing if his mother didn't stop pushing him, he would continue to reject marriage forever just to spite her. Which would be a travesty on many fronts. For Reese would make a wonderful husband and father, whether he was her husband or not. She'd hate for him to give up on a life of happiness just to win a war with the countess.

The other woman smiled. "Yes, one can hope." With that she picked up her needlepoint again and went back to work.

Harlow hoped this was not considered manipulation on her part. She only wanted him to be free of his mother's constant pressure so he could choose for himself. And now that Lady Breckenridge seemed to agree, Harlow could move on to the second part of her plan.

# Chapter Twenty-Six

I T HAD SEEMED like the longest of afternoons with Harlow spending the time in the drawing room with his mother. Reese had ledgers to look over and other things he could be doing, but instead he found himself staring out the window until it was time for supper.

He practically leapt from his chair, all the sooner to get to the dining room so he could see Harlow. He should have been seeking ways to distance himself from her. But as he'd tried that already, he knew it wouldn't make him want her any less. He was gone for the lass.

Which meant he would need to do something to secure a future with her. Something drastic like ask her to marry him. Again. And hope this time her answer would be different.

The meal was strange in that it was quieter. At least from his mother's front. She didn't seem resolved to push him into marriage by speaking of it every second of the time they were in a room together.

Instead she asked about the gardens and what flowers were there. She didn't even sneer at the dog who had lumbered into the room to curl up unobtrusively next to Harlow's chair.

He hoped the change was precipitated by her abandoning her marriage schemes once and for all.

The conversation went from the gardens to discussions in the House of Lords and Reese's earlier efforts to get bills passed to help in the recovery of lands to Scots. It had been a great success with his friends at his side leading the charge.

Whether the other lords agreed or were simply intimidated by the three large Scots, Reese couldn't be sure, but he didn't much care if it resulted in getting the votes he'd needed.

"Will you play for us this evening?" his mother said. He glanced up to tell her he had other plans for the evening, when he saw she was looking directly at him.

"Me?"

"Yes. You play the pianoforte beautifully."

Reese looked to the side thinking perhaps there was someone standing behind him that played the pianoforte beautifully. But no, it was only him. Unless, she meant Reggie the footman who had already moved away.

"Me?" he repeated, just to be sure because the idea was ludicrous.

"Yes. I know it's been some time—"

"Some time? Mother I haven't touched a piano since I was a lad of ten." This wasn't entirely true for just a few days before he'd ushered Harlow into the music room when his mother had gone upstairs for a nap, and taken Harlow on the very instrument. Meaning, he'd most definitely touched it. Though he'd never admit as much to his mother.

"That's a shame. You were so good."

She had never said anything encouraging about his playing. Hell, she rarely praised him for anything.

"What are you playing at mother?" he blurted, hoping his bluntness would shock her into telling the truth.

"I'm sure I don't know what you mean. I remember you playing quite well, and I never had to lecture you about practicing, which meant you must have liked playing. If I am wrong about that, then please accept my apologies for misinterpreting it."

He scowled at his roast as he tried to puzzle out what was happening. Had his mother been switched out with an imposter? If so, he needed to thank the person because this version was much better.

"In truth, I did enjoy it a lot. But in school, I was encouraged to put it aside to learn more important things. Like how to properly manage my lands and how parliament worked." He looked up with a smile. "Very important, indeed, but not as much fun as playing."

His mother gave a nod before speaking.

"Now that you have mastered all the things you needed to learn back then, you could return to the things you did for enjoyment, could you not? After all, finding happiness in the arts is just as important as making a profit. It is rather a profit for your soul."

His gaze narrowed on his mother again as he studied her. But she didn't look up from her plate to meet his eyes. Either she was quite interested in the food she regularly criticized or she was up to something.

Whatever it was, he could play along until she gave herself away. As he usually did when conversing with her, he looked out ahead of the conversation to predict her next move. Much like a person does when playing an opponent in chess. But this game was much more important because one false step and Reese could give up the entire game.

And then he saw it. Her plan. Did she think he would not see her manipulations so easily? Once he agreed to take up playing the piano again, she would likely request Harlow as a teacher, hoping to force them into close proximity where they might fall in love and marry.

Well, he would put a stop to that immediately.

He took another bite and stopped chewing abruptly when he considered the plan as if it had been his rather than his mother's. He found it to be sound.

If Harlow could see that softer side of him, something else

they shared that she loved, perhaps it would help him in winning her over.

But if his mother suggested it, he wouldn't be able to agree for it would be seceding too much. He couldn't allow her to manipulate him.

"Perhaps, someday, I might wish to play again. For now, I am quite busy with other things."

Harlow casually set down her fork and turned to him.

"If you would like, I'd be happy to instruct you. I taught Thomas, and he has very little patience for sitting and learning something from his younger sister. Still, he was able to play a few songs when we were finished. If I can teach him, I would think teaching you—someone who already has played, and doesn't wish to run off when something else grabs your attention— would be quite easy, indeed."

"That is kind of you, Lady Harlow," his mother said with a smile. "But you will likely be gone home when the earl wishes to pick up the instrument again. Besides, you are a lady, not a pianoforte instructor. It wouldn't be proper."

"Yes, of course," Harlow agreed and bowed her head some- what as if she were embarrassed for having suggested such a scandalous affair as teaching someone how to properly place their fingers on the keys.

"As we have all established, I do know how to play. There- fore, I wouldn't need an instructor. If I only need someone to remind me of the fundamentals, it would not be improper for Lady Harlow to assist."

His mother gave a demure shrug.

"You shall do whatever you wish anyway. Pay me no mind. Proper or no, I will report to everyone whatever you want me to say." She returned her attention to her plate and muttered what was obviously loud enough to be heard, "Not that I have a choice in the matter."

Reese might have felt guilty for dictating what she did by threatening her funds, if he were not so confused. She had relented.

She never backed away from badgering him when it was something she wanted him to do. What was going on here? Was the woman well? She was eating, and generally people who don't feel well lose their appetite first. Unless she was not well of mind. She was not that old, being years younger than his father. But perhaps she was muddled. For clearly she had forgotten their rules of engagement.

She pestered him to do something he didn't want to do, and he obstinately refused until she gave up. But now she was suggesting he not do something he wanted to do. It seemed that he would have to show her he was the victor by doing just that.

He turned to Harlow with a smile.

"I would appreciate it, if you would spend some time with me this evening as I muddle my way through some songs at the pianoforte."

Harlow fairly beamed with excitement and nodded.

"Of course, my lord. I would be happy to help."

So it was that after the meal was over he and Harlow went to the music room while his mother shook her head in disapproval and returned to her needlepoint in the drawing room.

He had won.

Or so he thought, until he found himself sitting next to Harlow, playing a horrid rendition of the *Fatted Goose is Dead* and wishing he'd remembered that he hadn't liked playing as much as he'd thought. Especially when his instructor was so very lovely.

Every time he attempted to distract her with kisses, she pushed him back.

"We can't. Not when we are supposed to be playing. Don't you think your mother will grow suspicious if there is no music coming from this room?"

"Hell," he cursed in complaint, for this plan had completely blown back on him. Still, if the instrument needed to make noise, it could surely make better sounds if they came from someone other than him.

"Why don't you play, and I'll watch. That will help a great

deal with finger placement and..." He searched his mind for another musical term. "Timing," he finally supplied.

"Very well." She smirked at him, as if she knew what he was up to.

She played for another half an hour and they decided that was enough. His mother had surely retired for the evening. Which meant they could do the same. Only instead of going to sleep they could be together. Alone.

He led her upstairs and after darting a glance down the hall to his mother's closed door they shared a kiss filled with promises of more to come. When he released her, she turned and hurried to her room, looking over her shoulder with a tempting smile.

Shaking his head, he turned for his own room so he might change into something more comfortable and less inhibiting.

When he was changed, he stood by the door waiting. And waiting. They'd forgot to discuss which room they would meet in. Was she to come to his or was he to go to hers as he had the night before?

Unable to wait another minute, he left the room and was halfway down the hall when Harlow left her own room, bidding Belle to stay inside. When she turned to see him, she smiled and walked slowly in his direction.

He opened his mouth to suggest they go back to his room, but she stood on tiptoe to kiss him, right there in the hall. It seemed she was as ravenous for him as he was for her. He took control of the kiss. Pushing her against the wall until she reciprocated, his back pressed against a painting of his great grandfather.

He was again ready to suggest they take things to his room rather than risk being caught in the hall together when she was only wearing a nightgown and he wrapped loosely in his banyan. But she retreated away from him, pulling him along.

He smiled, glad she'd had the same idea, but instead of leading him by the hand to his room, she spun to take her turn with her back against the wall. Except there was not a wall there. In its place was an alcove, adorned with a small table and a vase of flowers.

He saw what was going to happen before it transpired, for it was clear there was to be a catastrophe, but while his mind responded quickly, his body was quite slower. So slow in fact, he was unable to stop the motion.

Harlow stumbled backward, bumping the table with a great force, which knocked the vase off the surface. Had it landed on the carpet stretched the length of the hall, it would have muffled the sound. But the alcove was not carpeted. So when the vase hit the floor, it did so with a loud crash.

He and Harlow seemed frozen as they both looked toward his mother's room. For a beat of his heart, he thought all would be fine. But only a second later, the door opened.

It seemed they were well and truly caught this time. It was only then that he realized there had been a trap at all, and Harlow had been the one to set it.

## Chapter Twenty-Seven

HARLOW DIDN'T KNOW what had happened. One moment she was kissing Reese and playing a fun game of taking control, when she inadvertently stumbled into a table, sending the vase crashing to the floor. A second later the door to the countess's room began to open, and in a blur she was inside a dark bed chamber with Reese's palm coving her mouth.

"Shh," he ordered with his other hand still grasping her arm.

She nodded to indicate she understood and would remain quiet but he didn't remove his hand. He could not see her, but surely he could have felt her nod. Eventually, when it seemed he wouldn't let go, she stepped back and did it for him.

"Don't make a sound," he said in a sharp hiss. Gone was the fun-loving earl who was kissing her in the hallway. In his place was a man who seemed quite angry. She couldn't see his face in the darkness of the room, but she felt how tense he was.

She remained quiet as they heard the countess speaking to a footman she'd retrieved to clean up the mess. They waited long after the corridor had fallen silent again.

Reese stepped to the window and opened it with a shove of the drapes and turned back to her. It took a second or two of seeing his fuming glare before she realized she was correct about him being furious and that it appeared he was mad at her.

"What have you done?" he asked, his voice still low and irate.

"Me? I accidentally knocked over a vase," she explained though wasn't certain why she had to. He had been there. He saw what happened. He'd saved them from being caught, but now he was mad.

Eventually the pieces fell into place.

"You think I did it on purpose," she said; there was no need to ask the question.

"In all the nights you've come to my room, you've never delayed in the hall because we both knew doing so presented too great a risk with my mother at the other end of the corridor. But tonight… I knew something was off with her from the conversation at dinner. She didn't try to manipulate me into doing what she wanted. I should have known."

She blinked at him. In complete shock that he would think such a thing of her.

"You think I devised this plan to be caught, so I could trap you into marriage? When I have told you repeatedly I would never marry under such conditions."

"So you've said. But it could have all been part of your plan to catch me off guard."

A cold laugh burst from her as she threw her hands up. "I can't believe this. You were kissing me in the hall. Perhaps you are the one who was trying to trap me."

"Lower your voice, unless you still intend for us to be caught here."

She was at a loss as to what to do. He'd been hunted by the misses and mamas of the ton and now he thought her to be like them. She couldn't think of any way to convince him it wasn't true.

But she lowered her voice because despite what he believed, she didn't wish for them to be caught. Reese only had so much control over his mother. It was one thing for him to demand she tell everyone nothing had happened between them when she had no proof. But yet another if the countess found them dressed as they were well after everyone had gone to bed.

"Very well," she whispered. "I will keep my voice down. But you are mad if you think I would devise such a plan."

"Am I? I want nothing more to believe it was only an accident, but it just seems all too perfect."

It was her turn to shush him when his voice grew louder. She pulled him away from the door, closer to the corner where they would be less likely to be heard.

"Tell me you and my mother did not plot your conspiracies this afternoon while in the drawing room."

She paused in her answer, as she recalled what they'd discussed—or not directly discussed—that afternoon. Harlow had, in fact, conspired with the countess so she would stop being an obstacle. But not this...

Her delay in responding sealed her fate. For he pulled away from her, hurt and betrayal in his dark eyes.

"It's not as you think," she said quickly in an attempt to defend herself. But it was too late.

Reese shook his head.

"Stay away from me. I can't believe ye—someone who has been betrayed by someone ye loved—would do the very thing to someone else."

With that he stole from the room, leaving her there alone in the dark. After checking the hallway and finding it empty, she scurried across the hall to her room. Belle came to her instantly and jumped up on the bed when Harlow flopped gracelessly on the mattress.

"He doesn't believe me," she told the dog as tears welled in her eyes. She lay there for a long time, recalling every action and word that transpired that evening. They'd been so happy and now it was all gone.

Some time, hours later as she was drifting off to sleep, she remembered something he'd said before he left. About how she had betrayed someone who loved her.

He loved her.

He'd surely not meant to admit such a thing when he was so angry, but the fact that he did, meant it was true.

He loved her.

And she loved him. She didn't know what could possibly come between them, but she realized she very much wanted to know. Which meant she needed to find a way to fix everything.

INSTEAD OF GOING back to his rooms, Reese had fled downstairs to his study where he kept the whisky. One dram led to the next and the next until he was rambling to the empty room like a mad man.

After spending a good bit of time accusing Harlow of duplicity and considering just when she'd begun her ruse.

"Mayhap she was never even aboard Merrick's ship. She may have just walked up the beach from another property and staged the whole thing. The strained ankle so I would have to carry her." He made a hmmph at that thought. "How had she known to mention Merrick's name? Or the Zephyr? Unless she is an agent."

He stood to pace but sat back down when he realized walking about was beyond him at the moment. Did he really believe everything between them had been false?

The way she liked Stonecliff novels was a bit too perfect as well. Wouldn't Belle have been able to detect deceit? Unless Belle wasn't Belle but another dog switched out with his loyal beast.

His thoughts were becoming more and more delusional by the moment. A fake dog?

And then he had to face the other facts he'd been careful not to consider before, for they were the most painful. Could she have been faking everything that had happened between them in bed?

When she'd looked up at him, trusting and open, had it all been part of her tricks to trap him?

He imagined she'd succeeded, for he had ruined her and he was a gentleman. Tomorrow, he would offer marriage, because it was expected of him. And while he would offer up his title, he wouldn't offer up his heart. Never again.

The next thought he had was why his staff was still working on those bloody stairs. Hadn't they finished them the day before? But now here they were banging about again when his head was a mess.

After some time, he eventually opened his eyes to find it was late in the morning. He could only be grateful for the clouds and drizzle that kept the sun from scalding his eyes with its brightness. He rubbed his neck, twisting it from side to side in an effort to get rid of the ache from falling asleep at his desk. He then realized the banging wasn't coming from outside but at the door.

"Enter," he yelled, much too loud for his aching head.

Finch came in looking sharp and clean as ever. He frowned at Reese's opposite state.

"A Mr. Calloway has arrived, my lord. I've seated him in the library and asked Mrs. Garrison to bring refreshments. I will ask her to see to some coffee for you first, my lord."

"Good," Reese said, thought he hadn't caught up to what he was agreeing to yet. His mind seemed a few steps behind this morning.

Mrs. Garrison bustled in with a tray.

"I've brought you coffee and a bit of dry toast to help with your stomach."

The fact that his staff knew exactly how to handle his hard mornings proved he'd had too many of them. He couldn't help but think this time it was warranted, however. It wasn't every day that a man found out the woman he loved had betrayed him.

He stopped with the cup raised halfway to his lips.

Good God. Had he said those words last night? He'd admitted that he loved her without realizing it. She must have been ecstatic with the news she had lured him into her trap.

"If there's nothing else, I must see to Lady Harlow. The lass is having an ill morning as well. She says her puffy eyes are from the gardens, but I've seen the effects of spending the night in tears. I'm guessing she's missing her family. Poor girl."

Harlow had been crying? She'd not spent the night rejoicing for having won the game?

Perhaps there was no game at all? Mayhap he was wrong about everything. If the vase had truly been an accident…

"Bloody hell," he whispered.

"What's that, m'lord?"

"Nothing, Mrs. Garrison. Thank you."

She nodded and left the room. Reese rose and when he wobbled and felt his stomach lurch, he reached for the toast and another swig of coffee. It wouldn't do for him to go to Harlow's room with green gills to get to the bottom of things.

After he'd finished the meager breakfast, he stood to head for the door only to be met by Finch again.

"Did ye forget about Mr. Calloway?"

Reese blinked, for he had indeed forgotten about the stranger now waiting for him in his library. Very well. He'd see to his visitor, then bathe and dress before going to Harlow to beg an apology.

Reese stepped into the library and stopped, taking in the man seated by the window.

"Hello *Mr. Calloway*," Reese said, knowing the man's real name was Lord Collins, the Marquess of Evershire, and agent for the Home Office. "What the blazes are you doing here?"

Reese didn't care for the man. He'd proven himself a reckless agent. Reese thought him responsible for another agent's death, but had not been able to prove it.

"There has been a change of plans."

"I assure you, there can be no *change* of plans for me as I wasn't involved in any of the plans in the first place." Reese flopped down in the seat across from him. "Albert is seeing to Merrick."

"Albert is reporting to me now. Like I said, there's been a

change. He's coming here."

Reese didn't have time for any of this. He had a woman to puzzle out. It seemed a difficult task indeed, but he needed to know if she'd been manipulating him. And if she hadn't…

Well, if she proved true, he'd not be a coward any longer. He would tell her how he felt about her and then he hoped she felt the same.

"Albert was already here and interrogated Lady Harlow. He knows everything. So if you'll excuse—"

"Not Albert. Damn, but your head is as much a mess as your attire this morning, Breckenridge. Merrick. That's who's coming here."

Reese's eyes went wide as he nearly shrieked at the man. "He can't come here! Harlow is here!"

"Exactly."

In that moment, Reese would have loved to pour a stout glass of whisky to handle the situation. But being that he still had the good part of a bottle sloshing about in his brain and gut, he needed to remain lucid so he could fix this mess.

"I don't understand. We told Albert that Merrick would be in port in Inverness. Why did you not go there and seize the bastard?"

"That was the original plan. But when we arrived in Inverness, we couldn't find him. The bastard is a ghost for everyone had seen him, but no one knew where he was."

"Couldn't find him? For Christ's sake, Collins, the Zephyr is a fair size ship. How could you miss it? Sails, red as blood, and a bare-chested woman on the bow carrying a rabbit, for what reason I cannot fathom."

"We know what his bloody ship looks like, but it wasn't there."

"Then perhaps he is heading back to London. You can head him off there."

"We don't think he's returning to London. Word got out he is being charged with treason. Merrick was still in Inverness, but the Zephyr is anchored somewhere else. That's when I decided to lure him to a place of my choosing rather than hunting him down."

"No. It is too risky. I'll not have Harlow put in danger."

"It's too late. We've already spread word through Inverness of a dark-haired woman washing up on shore at Slains Castle. Alive, but having lost her memories. I even put up a drawing of her on posters looking for her family. He'll be coming here, trying to get her and finish out his plan to use her. And then we'll have him."

"You're planning to use an innocent lass as bait to lure a known killer and traitor to the Crown? I know you have stooped to disreputable dealings in the past, but this is too much, Collins. I'll not have it."

"As I said, it's too late. He's coming. Besides, I knew you'd want to be the one to bring him in after what he did to you. You'll finally have your revenge."

Revenge? Yes, he'd wanted it many times. Envisioned bringing the man to justice so maybe his dreams would no longer be haunted by the whoreson. He'd wished for the man to be there before him every night Reese had woken choking for breath from a nightmare. He could have easily strangled the life from the blighter with his bare hands. But not now. Not when Harlow was here. She'd given him peace and comfort. He'd not allow her to be put in danger like this.

"No. You'll find a way to fix this. Go back to Inverness and tell all who will hear that the girl passed away from her injuries. Do it. Go now."

"Even if I were to do such a thing, Captain Merrick would never hear it for I'm sure he's already on his way here."

"How long?" Reese asked, and Collins didn't need to clarify what he was asking.

"A day, maybe two at the most, and this will all be over. We'll grab him up before he even has the chance to see Harlow Haverston. I promise she will not be in any harm."

But he could not make such promises. Men like Merrick didn't sashay into traps. Reese, himself, had been told he was not in any danger from Merrick that night on the dock, but the bullet searing through his leg had proved otherwise.

If Merrick was coming here, Reese would need to take Harlow away to safety. Maybe Shay's or Finn's. His friends would take her in and protect her.

Reese might have yelled or even punched the man who had put her in such danger, except for a knock at the door.

"No refreshments for Mr. Calloway, Mrs. Garrison. The man was just leaving."

"Sorry, my lord, but you have another guest."

# Chapter Twenty-Eight

R EESE'S MUDDLED HEAD was not up for the task of dealing with all the horrors of a day that had begun hours before him.

"Who has arrived?" Reese snapped as his blood went cold and his stomach twisted. Surely Merrick wouldn't have the cods to waltz into Reese's home as an invited guest.

"Lady Harlow's brother and uncle have arrived, my lord."

They had a plan for this. The whole house was ready for this moment. But they hadn't anticipated that a killer would be arriving at the same time.

"You're certain, we have a day at least?" Reese barked at the man across from him. If he had a day or two before Merrick showed up, he would have time to assist Harlow with her plans and still get her away from Slains Castle before Merrick arrived.

"At least."

Turning back to a confused Mrs. Garrison he asked, "Have you told her yet?"

"Not yet. I came directly to you. She's still in her room. I put our guests in the morning room as planned."

"My mother?"

"Is in the drawing room."

"Go assist Harlow and ready the house."

When Mrs. Garrison left the room in a hurry, Reese turned back to Collins and shook his head.

"I hope to God you're wrong and Merrick has given up on this plot. For if he hurts her, I will gut ye. This is not how honorable men keep the citizens of Great Britain safe, and you well know it. You stay here until I return. I must go wake the dead."

Leaving the study, Reese slipped into the drawing room.

"There you are, Reese," his mother said before looking up from her needlepoint. She tilted her head. "Are you well? You look dreadful."

"It was a bad night."

"Perhaps you've caught whatever ails Lady Harlow, for she is not well this morning either."

His mother was likely more correct than she knew.

"I'm sorry, Mother, I haven't time to discuss this. Her uncle has arrived."

His mother's eyes went wide with surprise before she nodded.

"I'm ready." His mother had been given a small part in this scheme. She would no doubt play it to perfection. Her brother had been sent instructions as well. They could only hope his acting skills were convincing.

His mother rushed over to the corner to grab up a lace veil and drape it over her shoulders, covering her midnight blue gown in black.

When she looked the picture of grief, she took his arm so he could lead them off to the first scene of their play.

"Let us go greet our guests," he said.

"This should be great fun," his mother said.

He was glad someone was looking forward to this. Reese knew when all of this was over, there would be no reason for Harlow to stay with him. He didn't know what would happen then.

HARLOW WAS SITTING by the window looking out at the back gardens and the ocean beyond. She'd dried her tears hours before dawn and had a plan to speak to Reese. She had just lacked the courage to go down to see him as yet.

It was after noon and she was still hiding out in her room, the gloom of the day directly reflecting her mood. She didn't yet know what words to say to convince the man she loved that he was wrong and she loved him.

She thought it might be better to hide away in her room until she was certain his mood had improved. She knew from experience that giving her father time to calm down made his punishments easier.

While she didn't expect Reese to punish her, she still needed him to be in a better mood than he'd been when he'd run off the night before.

At the swift knock at her door, she frowned. Mrs. Garrison had already brought a tray of food that sat untouched on the table by the door. Harlow hadn't had an appetite that morning with all the worrying.

When the knock came again, Harlow wondered if it was Reese.

She stood.

"Come in," she called.

When the door opened and Mrs. Garrison came in, Harlow had to work hard to hide her disappointment. But then she spotted the dress in the woman's arms.

"They have arrived, m'lady. It's time."

Harlow jumped into action.

"Is everyone ready?"

"Yes. The earl and the countess have gone to the morning room to meet our guests. We must hurry so you can get out to the gardens." They'd chosen to put her uncle in the morning room rather than the drawing room as it faced the other side of the house from the gardens.

After the gown was in place, Mrs. Garrison went to work on her hair and the rest of her disguise.

"These red eyes of yours are at least good for something. You look like death." The woman tutted her disapproval. "The earl looked like a man in mourning before your uncle even arrived."

"He did?"

"Aye. I don't know what the two of you are so broken up about, but I hope when this is over, you'll see to talking it out."

Reese was upset? Mrs. Garrison hadn't said he was angry.

"Yes. I promise we will do that. For now, though, I must terrorize the man who betrayed me until he wishes he'd never been born."

"I pray I never earn your ire, m'lady. Ye are a fierce one, indeed."

With a smile, Harlow hurried down the servant's stairs and rushed out to the gardens.

⟫⟪

As Reese escorted his mother into the morning room, the countess flew into hysterical tears.

"Too late! Too late! The poor dear has passed," his mother wailed, and he would applaud her later for such a convincing performance. She quieted only slightly before slumping into the nearest chair.

Reese turned a concerned look to the men as he gave them the grim news. He didn't know which brother had come, but he could tell the older of the two must be Edgar Polk. Reese reached out a hand.

"Welcome to Slains Castle, gentlemen. I'm sorry it couldn't be under better circumstances. I am Lord Breckenridge."

"Luke Haverston, and this is my uncle, Edgar Polk. I thank

you for finding my sister."

Luke was not so good an actor, for he was smiling instead of looking nervous or struck to hear his sister had died.

"Unfortunately, as my dear mother has said, it is too late. The lass passed peacefully nearly a week ago. I wrote, but of course, ye were already on your way here."

"Oh dear," Luke said and Reese wanted to pinch the man for not being more overcome. Fortunately, Edgar didn't notice for he had crumbled onto the settee and began sobbing in earnest.

"This is all my fault," he said over and over. Reese looked toward the doorway thinking Harlow would want to see the man's evident pain at hearing her dead. But she was likely in position for the next step of their plan. Which meant Reese needed to get them to their places.

"Mayhap you would like to see where she is buried. I wasn't able to have a stone carved with a name, as I didn't know it. It is only marked with a cross for now. But it may give ye peace to see it."

"Harlow, my lord. My sister's name was Harlow." Better. Luke was getting the hang of it now. "I would like to visit her grave and will see to the matter of having a proper stone cut."

"Aye. This way." Reese led them from the house, skirting the edge of the garden to the back corner where everything was prepared. There in the graveyard, where his own father was buried, there was a pile of dirt with a large wooden cross stuck in the ground. He and Harlow had had such a great laugh setting it up.

Walking over to the edge of the garden, he retrieved a few flowers and saw Harlow lurking behind a nearby tree. Even knowing it was powder and ash, he winced at seeing how close to death she looked. It was unsettling.

As he knelt to place the flowers reverently on the mound, he heard Polk gasp.

Looking at Luke, Reese silently reminded him with a stern glare to play his part well. It was no surprise the man was happy to be involved in a bit of mischief.

"She's there!" Polk cried out as he pointed to where Harlow was standing in a flowing white gown they had rent at the ends so it was tattered and what she had called "specter-like." Her eyes were rimmed in fireplace ash so they looked sunken into her pale white cheeks. Her lips were stained red with berries as she slowly raised her arm and pointed directly at Polk.

"This is *your* fault, Uncle," she spoke in a soft, eerie timbre.

"What is wrong, Uncle?" Luke said shaking his head.

"Do you not see her?" Edgar pointed as Luke looked to where the other man was pointing, not reacting to Harlow in the slightest. Either the man was getting better with his role or he was used to ignoring his sister.

"I don't see anything. Do you want me to pick more flowers?" Luke strode over directly next to Harlow and fetched a few blooms, still acting as if he didn't see her at all.

Harlow had said any one of her brothers would be up for such a role for they'd all played dead at some point in their youth. But it was another thing to see it.

"She is right there." The man pointed. "Harlow."

Luke spun around and then came closer to his uncle.

"Shh. There is nothing there. Relax. Harlow is with the angels now."

Harlow stepped closer to Polk.

"You did this to me, Uncle. I loved you and you allowed those men to take me. You told them they could have me. To do whatever they wanted with me."

"No!" he shouted. "I didn't. I swear it. It isn't my fault."

Reese looked at Harlow, knowing she would not be pleased that the man was still not admitting what he had done. His hideous part in the scheme to use his own flesh and blood for money.

"Yes!" she screamed back. "Tell the truth. Tell the truth right now. I cannot leave this realm until I know why I was left to die."

"God, forgive me. I didn't know. I didn't know he would do this."

"Confess all!" Harlow shouted and took a step closer. She was not playing the part, instead she was allowing her anger to take over.

"I didn't know," he said again. "I didn't know who he was. He said I could help him and make a fortune. I've never had anything of my own. My sister married your father and he has paid for everything I have since that day. And while I was grateful, I hated it all the same." The man let his head fall in his hands for a moment. "I wanted to have something of my own. I wanted to prove my own worth. So I said yes. But when he told me what he wanted me to do, I realized it would be treason. I was to go to a ball and steal documents from Lord Martindale's study. I found the documents he wanted. It was a list of all the agents of the Crown. I knew I couldn't trust a man such as Merrick with such a list. Instead of taking it, I tossed it into the fire."

"An honorable thing to do," Luke whispered to Reese without Polk or Harlow hearing. Reese had to admit it was not as they'd originally thought.

"Tell the truth! I was taken. Why was I taken? Why was I tied up and taken to Scotland?"

"Leverage," the man sobbed. "He knew I had seen the names. Even without the document I would know who they were and he planned to force me to tell him. When I didn't, he lost a great sum of money from the French who were willing to pay for the list. The amount was more than I could pay back. He told me he would be reimbursed for what he lost. I didn't know what he intended until that day in the park when they took you."

"You told them they could keep me!"

"No! I never agreed to anything. If I'd known they planned to take you, to hurt you, I would never have let you go to the park. I love you, Harlow."

"No, you don't!" she shouted. "You didn't do anything to stop them. You didn't help me. You let them take me."

She was crying now and the ash was running down her face. If Polk wouldn't have been in hysterics, he might have noted that specters didn't often have their face stream black like this. Of course, Reese had never seen a specter, so how was he to know for certain.

"I should have fought them. I should have stopped them. But there were so many—"

"You did nothing. You ran away like a coward and let them take me." Her voice had calmed slightly, but was all the scarier for the steadiness of it. "You will pay for what happened, Uncle."

With that she pulled a pistol from the billowing fabric hanging from her arms. Reese recognized it as being the one from his study. When had she taken it? More importantly, why? Ghosts didn't have much need for firearms. She'd wanted to frighten her uncle into admitting what he'd done, and they'd done that. This was not what they'd planned.

"Is this part of it?" Luke asked at Reese's side.

"Nay. We need to put a stop to this before she does something she'll regret."

"Good. Yes. You should go stop her," Luke said with a nod as he took a step back and then another.

Reese shook his head and turned to tell Harlow to put the gun down, but before he could, a shadow stepped out behind her and another pistol came into view. This one in the hand of bloody Captain Merrick.

❧ ⬥ ❧

# Chapter Twenty-Nine

H ARLOW BARELY FELT the cold barrel of the pistol at her temple. She had been so angry she worried she might catch fire with her hatred at any second. But now she had lost control of the situation.

"Let her go, Merrick," Reese said and Harlow felt her stomach lurch at the knowledge that the man holding a gun to her head was the man who'd had her taken from London in the first place. Only vaguely did she wonder how Reese knew the man by sight. But the fear had pushed away all thought but self-preservation.

"Ah, Breckenridge. I thought I killed you once but missed my mark. I won't make that mistake again."

Merrick was the man who had hurt Reese?

Her uncle looked up from where he had knelt on the ground begging for forgiveness from his dead niece. It was exactly what she had wanted, but it hadn't made her feel any better. She still hurt from the man's betrayal.

Now, Edgar blinked and looked around in confusion.

"You see her? She is alive?"

"For now," Merrick chuckled. "I have to say I was wondering what this performance was all about. I was quite entertained until she planned to kill the man who holds the names I need. The man who owes me for his disloyalty." He gave Harlow a pat. "Don't worry, love, I'll do away with him for you. But only after I get what I need first."

She thought she might be sick. All this time she'd been so angry at her uncle, blind with rage. And he had only been a pawn in Captain Merrick's plans. It was hard to let go of the anger she'd cloaked herself with all this time. But it had been misplaced. She should have been angry at Merrick. It was he who needed to pay.

Reese took a step closer and Merrick pulled Harlow closer.

"Stay back, unless you want to watch the girl's head get blown off. It would be a shame as I'd had other plans for her..." The man leaned down and sniffed her hair.

"Reese?" She didn't know what he could do, but she needed him.

"Aye, your hero and I have some business as well. Come. We'll sort everything out on the Zephyr."

She shoved at the large man but he didn't loosen his grip around her waist. The barrel of the pistol bit into her temple, causing her to whimper. She hated the sound of weakness coming from her throat, but there was nothing for it. She was defeated.

Suddenly a shot rang out and Merrick dropped behind her.

She lifted her head to see a stranger with a pistol step out and rush at Merrick, kicking the gun from his grip. The captain was shot in the shoulder and was still alive but moaning as he grasped his wound.

Then she was pressed against Reese's chest.

"Are you all right?" he asked.

She didn't know how to respond so she didn't.

"Good job, Reese. The plan worked perfectly," the other man said with a wide smile. "We finally got him, and you got your revenge on Merrick."

She was shaking as everything that had happened seemed to twist in on itself. It was all tied together in a huge knot of deceit.

"You used me to get to Merrick," she whispered. "You agreed to help me only to get what you wanted."

"No. Harlow. That's not—"

She pulled away from him and went to her brother.

"Take me home. I wish to be away from this place."

Fortunately, Luke didn't hesitate to do just that.

REESE RAN HIS hands through his hair as he watched the Ardmere carriage ride off with the woman he loved.

"The Home Office will hear about this, Breckenridge. You'll be up for a commendation. You assisted in capturing Merrick and now we have Polk's confession as well." Collins fairly gleamed with excitement, oblivious to how thoroughly Reese's world had just imploded.

Before the man got out another word, Reese strode to him and punched him right in the face, knocking him to his back there in the drive. He heard a low chuckle come from inside the carriage. Merrick was likely amused that his captor had been knocked from his senses.

Fortunately, both Merrick and Polk were chained in irons to the inside of the carriage where they would stay until they arrived back in London. When Collins came to a few moments later, he shook his head and sat up.

"What the bloody hell, Breckenridge?"

"I don't give a damn about any of this." He waved toward the carriage. The only thing Reese cared about had left him without giving him a chance to explain. "You put an innocent woman in danger. I will make sure the counsel hears of what measures you took to capture your target. This is not how a gentleman goes about these things."

"You were an agent yourself, so you know that sometimes people get hurt in order to protect the great good."

Reese lurched out, planning to strike the man again as the first time had obviously not helped him. Collins was ready this time and ducked away.

"If this about the girl, I'm sure she'll come around." The man rolled his eyes as if he didn't know how close he was to having the life choked from him. "Everyone knows you're a catch."

With that, the man jumped up into his carriage.

"Lord Breckenridge," Polk said, his face streaked with tears. When Reese's attention moved to him, the man continued. "Thank you for taking care of my niece. You don't know how relieved I am to know she is alive and safe. I am in your debt."

"Now that the truth has come out, Harlow may forgive you."

Polk frowned and shook his head. "I don't deserve her forgiveness. But I'll do whatever is needed to see this man can never harm her again."

He glared at Merrick seated next to him. It was clear that Polk would testify against Merrick and the captain would be hung for his crimes. But what would happen to Polk?

"See that he is given a chance," Reese said to Collins. He didn't know if or when Harlow would see the truth of Polk's involvement, but if she did, she wouldn't want to find out he was hung. That would likely weigh on her, and Reese wouldn't have it.

"Yes. It seems he's not as bad as we thought. That will be for the court to decide. Not me. We need to go."

With that, they rode off, leaving Reese standing there alone in his drive as the sky finally let loose with the rain.

Eventually, he made it into the house to find his mother waiting for him.

"You may return to London, Mother. You are no longer needed here. I'll see your accounts are paid."

"Reese? Are you well? I can stay—"

He didn't answer. He continued alone to his study and locked himself inside with a substantial amount of whisky.

LUKE TOOK HARLOW to their country home in Lancashire where her entire family was waiting. Well, not her entire family. Uncle Edgar was not there, and she doubted she would ever see him again. He'd been taken into custody with Merrick and would be tried for his involvement, which turned out to not be as she'd thought.

In fact, he'd done the right thing in getting rid of the list and keeping the information from falling into the hands of the French. And she wanted to believe he'd not known Merrick's plans to take her from the park that morning.

He'd been right when he'd said he couldn't have fought off so many of them. Yet, he hadn't even tried.

It was strange that she missed someone she'd thought to do away with by her own hand. But if she'd learned anything in all of this, it was that emotions didn't always make a bit of sense. For she also missed Reese, and he had used her to get his own revenge on the man who had tried to kill him.

Her brothers kept their distance, offering worried smiles when she made eye contact with them. Luke must have told them all that had transpired in Scotland and they either didn't know what to say or were terrified of her.

She didn't bother to do anything to ease the tension for she didn't know what to say to them either. She was angry at everyone, including herself. It was best for her to just stay in her room looking out the window at nothing.

"Dearest?" her mother called as she came into the room. "You need to eat something."

Harlow had been there for three days already and had barely eaten for fear she might not keep it down. Her appetite seemed to have remained at Slains Castle along with her heart. She was a mess of conflicting feelings. For even after Reese had betrayed her, she loved him still.

"He lied to me," Harlow said, breaking down into tears despite her aversion to crying. It did nothing to help a situation. She still felt awful.

"Shh…" Her mother sat next to her and pulled her into a hug much like she'd done when Harlow was small and she'd been upset over her brothers leaving her behind. "I'm sorry, pet. I know you are hurting, but I'm so glad to have you here. Safe and sound. You don't need to worry about anything that happened in Scotland. You never need to think on it again."

"I loved him," Harlow confessed. "And he lied."

"I know. I did as well. I never thought my own brother was capable of such a betrayal. He will pay for his mistakes."

Her mother thought she was overwhelmed with everything that had happened, and in truth, she was. But this heartache was not because of her uncle.

"I was speaking of Lord Breckenridge."

"Oh. I see." Her mother looked out the window in surprise before tilting her head and smiling. "Love?"

"Please do not plan to have the banns read, Mother. He doesn't wish to marry. And he was not the man I thought he was."

"Because he lied?"

"The whole time I was there he was using me to lure Captain Merrick to him so he could retaliate for being shot."

"It does sound like there was an awful lot of revenge going about in Scotland. Luke said you turned a pistol on Edgar. While I would gladly beat the man to his reward with my hat, that is not like you, Harlow."

"I thought he'd betrayed me. While he was a coward, I don't think he meant for me to be harmed. He did not handle things well at all, but at least he did not use me merely for bait."

"We're speaking of Lord Breckenridge again?"

Harlow could understand why her mother was confused. For Harlow was tossing back and forth in conversation.

"Yes. I thought he cared for me. I was foolish to think a man would do anything without gaining something from it. I was simply a part of his plan. Nothing more."

"But you love him?" Her mother seemed fixated on that one part of the story.

"Only because I can't seem to make myself angry enough to stop. I'm sure in a few days I'll manage to forget all about him." Even as she said it, she doubted it would be true. She wanted to see him. She wanted to yell at him. She wanted to kiss him. My she was a paradox, if ever she'd known one.

"And you're certain he doesn't care for you? From what Luke said the man went out of his way to assist you with your plan to..." Her mother coughed and let out a breath. "Well, I'm not exactly sure what transpired, but I'm to believe you were dressed up as a specter to force Edgar into confessing to his crimes..."

"Aye—I mean, *yes*." She placed her fingertips to her lips as if to check to make sure they belonged to her. When had she taken to using Scottish words? Perhaps when she'd allowed a Scot to claim her lips so thoroughly. Clearing her throat, she attempted again. "Yes. If I was able to scare him a fraction as much as the fear I felt waking up on the Zephyr, then I thought to feel better about the ordeal."

"And do you? Feel better?" her mother asked.

That was a good question. One Harlow avoided answering for she didn't know how. She thought revenge would ease the hurt. She thought leaving Reese behind would ease the pain. So far, neither proved true. Instead of sharing all of that, she focused on the one small truth she could grasp onto.

"It is good to be home," she said instead, but even that didn't feel entirely right. She loved their manor house in the country, but it seemed too quiet now.

She'd grown accustomed to hearing the waves crash against the rocky shore. She often wondered if she was hearing the actual sound or echoes from past waves. More than just hearing was the way the house itself seemed to hum in rhythm to the sea that touched its very foundation. She felt as if she too had been shaken to her foundation. And now she must find a way to move forward.

"I plan to marry next year. The first suitable man who pro-poses will be my husband. It is time." She would give up on all the criteria she'd added to her original promise. So long as he wasn't a lying agent for the Crown, or a nefarious sea captain, she would make the match.

When her mother didn't speak, Harlow looked to see her staring at Harlow in surprise.

"What is it? It's not so strange. I've planned to marry since my first Season. I've just been too particular in the past. Actually, no it was not my doing. The boys found fault in every man who came near me. But this time, my brothers will have no say in the matter. In fact, I don't even want to speak to them about it. They have interfered long enough."

Her mother laughed softly. "I wondered when you would see what they were about."

"You knew they were toying with me?"

"I wouldn't say they were toying with you, Harlow. They love you and they show how they care about you by protecting you. Though probably protecting you more than is needed. But they are men, dear. Men have no mind for nuance." She waved a hand.

"If they truly wanted me to be happy, they would have guided me to a friend of theirs that was worthy, and I would already be married with a family. I wouldn't be so very alone with no prospects. I wouldn't have already..." Harlow hated that her eyes seemed to have sprung tears yet again, and her throat squeaked with tightness. For all the years she'd not cried it seemed to be catching up with her now.

"You wouldn't already have given your heart to another?" At her mother's correct assumption, Harlow could not keep the pieces together anymore. She broke down in loud, ugly sobs as her mother pulled her close.

When Harlow was able to speak, she nodded.

"Even if he had not used me to seek revenge, he doesn't wish to marry."

Her mother laughed and Harlow wasn't used to her mother being unkind.

"I'm sorry," her mother said only slightly gaining control of her mirth. "It is just that every man says that. Your father didn't wish to marry when he met me. David didn't wish to marry until he met Tabitha. Your other brothers do not wish to marry, but I daresay, they will seek out a wife eventually. It is the way of men at a certain age to fight it. Don't put much stock in such a declaration."

Harlow considered her mother's words. It was true enough that Harlow had said she hadn't wanted to marry someone because of a compromising situation, but she had fallen in love with Reese who had certainly compromised her in many different situations over the time she'd been at his home.

"Well, whether Lord Breckenridge has changed his mind, he hasn't asked for my hand." At least not lately. At least not when he meant it. Harlow wiped at the new tears that escaped.

"If he did, would you accept?"

Harlow didn't know the answer. Now that she'd had some time to think, she wasn't sure Reese had feigned his feelings for her when he'd taken her to his bed. Or during all the times they'd spent talking in his gardens or the looks and laughter they shared while reading to one another.

Rather than get into that, Harlow merely shrugged. Perhaps the man did care about her, and this scheme to use her for revenge was something he couldn't pass on when it presented itself.

Still, he'd put her in danger. How much could he care if he'd done that.

When the silence continued, her mother patted Harlow on the leg. "Give it more time. You may find that you are capable of forgiving him for his thoughtlessness. If you can, you will be well-suited for marriage. For there is a lot of forgiveness to be given—and received—in a marriage. Men are rather mutton-headed at times. It's best you know that going into the endeavor."

Harlow smiled at her mother and felt somewhat better.

Soon after her mother left, her brother knocked at the door.

"How are you?" Luke asked.

Harlow shrugged. "I'm in love with a man who used me as a pawn in his game of revenge. That is not a great thing to be."

He frowned. "I think you might be wrong about that, Lo."

"How so?"

"It's just that as we were leaving, I saw him punch Lord Collins, laying him out right there in the drive. I didn't understand it at first, but having had some time to think about it and what he said when we were leaving. Or rather tried to say, I think you might have it wrong. I think all this mess with Merrick showing up was Lord Collins's doing, not Breckenridge. He looked truly terrified when Merrick grabbed you."

"Perhaps I was hasty in leaving without allowing him to explain?" she said it as a question, hoping someone would tell her what to do.

"It would not be the first time you've jumped to conclusions and run off without giving the innocent party a chance to defend their actions."

"I know you are likely referring to the time you forgot to come look for me in the orchard, Luke Haverston, and I was not wrong in that matter."

They laughed together for a moment but when silence fell, she ran a hand over her skirt.

"Perhaps I did rush out of there rather quickly. Without giving the man a chance to explain."

"Perhaps," Luke allowed. "There is one way to find out."

"YOUR PRESENCE IS requested for the noon meal, m'lord," Finch said from the doorway of Reese's study.

Reese frowned at the idea of eating. His poor stomach had taken a great amount of abuse from his efforts to rid the castle of every drop of whisky in the last three days. And his sour stomach was only second to his aching head.

"Rupert has drawn a bath."

It didn't take skills in deciphering coded messages to understand that his staff thought he smelled bad.

"Who has requested my presence?" Reese asked, knowing he was the only one in the castle besides the staff.

"Lady Breckenridge."

Reese's eyes squinted in the direction of his butler.

"My mother is still in residence? I thought she would have fled for London the moment her duties were completed."

"Nay, m'lord. I believe she is concerned. As we all are."

Belle barked as if to say she was also concerned. She had not moved from her post by his side except for a few trips out to see to nature's call.

"Very well. I guess I shall bathe and dress for luncheon." It wasn't that he wished to do any of those things, but he couldn't keep on as he had been. He would soon grow concerned himself.

Perhaps he would make a good showing at the meal so his mother could go on her way, and then Reese could visit Shay or Finn. Some time away from Slains would do him well. It was as if the castle held tight to the specter of Harlow. Though she was not a ghost, pretend or otherwise, she haunted him still.

Reese felt some bit better as he came down from his room. His head and stomach still complained, but it was surely nothing a meal and some coffee would not quell.

His mother was already seated when he arrived.

"You look somewhat better," she said.

"I feel better. Somewhat."

"Do you?" she asked tilting her head.

"I'm working on it," he admitted. "It will take some time to mend everything." His heart had shattered and he wasn't certain he still owned all the pieces needed to make it whole again.

"You miss her," his mother stated as the meal was served.

Reese drank down half the cup of coffee before responding with a shrug.

"We knew it was only temporary."

His mother set down her cutlery rather loudly and huffed.

"You are a fool if you do not plan to do something to win the girl back."

"She doesn't wish to marry me," Reese defended.

"And you know this because you asked her?"

"I did. Or rather I attempted to. Once." He didn't need to go into the details. The point was that Harlow had rejected him.

"Had you asked immediately after you compromised her? Women don't like feeling like a responsibility."

Reese's eyes shot wide, which did not help his head.

"Whatever do you mean?" he attempted to defend her accusations, but his mother only waved him off.

"Please. I heard the woman sneaking out of your chambers nearly every night. It was as if you were on your honeymoon for as often as she visited. And that's not even considering the night you knocked over the vase."

"Had you planned to catch us?"

"Of course not. You were both just terribly bad at sneaking about."

"You didn't say anything. I would have thought—"

"That I would have called you out and forced you to wed the girl? We both know that method did not go well for either of us. You refused and I lost your trust. Besides, I didn't think I would have to resort to such machinations, for you love her and she loves you."

"But she hates me."

"Pish. She doesn't hate you. It was a blow for her to think you had used her, but you must tell her the truth. Make sure she hears *all* of your truth. She will forgive you. I'm sure of it."

"You seem to know a lot more about the situation than I have confessed to."

"It was easy enough to see." Again her mother waved, but this time it was toward the door to the terrace where Belle stood looking out and whining. "Go take your dog for her walk by the shore and when you come back we will plan what is to be done next."

He'd barely had time to finish his toast before she was waving the footmen to take the meal away.

As soon as he opened the terrace doors, Belle ran for the path that went down the cliff to the shore. Sometimes he wondered if the dog could actually understand complete conversations.

His mother was right though, the walk was good for clearing his head. The sea air gave it a right scrubbing as he made his way down the stairs to the sand strewn with rocks and boulders.

Belle rushed over carrying a stick, and Reese threw it as far as he could so the dog could get a good run. But as she raced up the shore, she abandoned her plan for the stick and instead turned barking toward a rock.

"Belle! Don't try to eat anything you find on the beach!" He reminded the dog as he picked up his pace to stop her from doing something they would both regret.

But when he made it to the dog, he stopped still when a dark-haired woman stepped out from behind the rock where Belle was excitedly wagging her tail.

"Harlow," he whispered. Unlike the last time his dog found her, she was awake and dressed properly. Her hair had been done as well, but the wind had tugged a number of strands free that were dancing around her smiling face.

"You're here." He wanted to rush forward and take her in his arms, but he needed to be sure she would want such a reunion first. For now he was just glad she was here. That he might have a chance to make things right again.

"In the flesh," she said, gesturing down at herself. "As opposed to the last time you saw me when I was a ghost." She laughed and he smiled, still in shock that she was there before him. But since she was, he rushed to explain what he had not had the chance to that evening.

"Harlow, I'm so sorry about what happened. I shouldn't have accused you of manipulating me into marriage. I know that wasn't what you wanted. And I didn't use you to lure Merrick here. I swear it. I never would have risked your safety like that."

"I know. I'm to understand Lord Collins conceived that horrid plan. And that is the reason you planted him a facer?" She tilted her head.

"You saw?"

"No. But Luke did and told me I might have been hasty to judge the situation." She rolled her eyes. "He was pleased to accompany me to the Home Office where I learned the truth. You'll be happy to know Lord Collins has been reprimanded and dismissed from his duties. And then Luke was all too happy to see me here so he could be proven right."

"I'm sure it happens so seldom…"

To this she laughed and he just watched as her green eyes glittered in happiness. He never thought he'd see her again let alone happy. Unable to wait another moment, he hurried to take up the distance between them. Holding her close.

"Luke is probably telling your mother all about it at the moment. I'm guessing she will be pleased to have tricked you into coming down here."

"Another plan to put me in a compromising position, I see."

"Yes, well I hope it is not in vain, for I have informed you of my wish to marry, and while I would have found the patience needed to wait until next Season to select a suitor, it turns out I am desperately in love with you and wish to marry only you."

"I don't think that's true," he said and when her eyes narrowed she shook her head.

"I assure you I am in love with you, Reese."

"Not about that. About you having enough patience to wait until spring to launch your attack on London's eligible bachelors."

She pressed her lips together as to keep from smiling but barely managed.

"Very well, I'll allow that. Still, it doesn't change anything. You are here instead of London. And since you have already proposed once—"

"Half proposed."

"Fine," she said, her smile growing wider. "I would like to ask you this time. It seems only fair."

When she waited, he backed up and tilted his head.

"Was this the part where you were going to ask? You only said you wanted to."

She let out an impatient sigh and scrunched up her nose. "You are quickly coming to the edge of my patience, sir."

He laughed. "I didn't know you had any patience to speak of, my lady." He took her hands in his, placing kisses on each of the knuckles. He enjoyed seeing the way her eyes flared with interest as his lips hesitated against her skin longer with each touch.

"Will you marry me, Reese? Not because we have found each other in a compromising situation and must wed, but because I love you and wish to spend the rest of my life with you?"

"It would seem despite our attempts, my mother has caught us out. She knows you visited my chamber for nefarious reasons. I really have no choice but to marry you to save our reputations."

Her brow creased and she shook her head.

"And that is the reason you will accept my suit?"

"Oh, hell no. I don't give a damn what my mother has seen or heard. I'm accepting because I love you more than anything and was prepared to track you down and make you listen to the truth until you agreed to marry me."

"The truth being that you love me?" she said, with a smug grin on her lips.

He could not be judged for having to kiss her then. And kiss her he did. Thoroughly until they were both gasping for air.

"Yes, I will marry you." He couldn't believe she had asked him, but it went a long way to healing his wounded ego from the previous rejections. This was the proposal that was most important, no matter who offered it.

"Soon?" she pressed.

"Now you're just getting pushy," he teased.

She ignored him and went on with her plan. "We are in Scotland where it is customary to marry immediately, and as you so rudely pointed out, I have very little patience."

"I said you have no patience whatsoever."

"Even more reason to marry me today. This instant."

"Then please stop standing around. Let's go back to the castle and ready my mother and future brother-in-law so they can accompany us to the nearest blacksmith. I cannot believe I am being forced to wait so long to marry you."

"Hmm... perhaps I know a way you might get revenge for my delay."

He ravished her lips and when he'd left her swaying, he smiled his most devilish grin. "I shall have my revenge, my lady. For the rest of our days."

❦

# Epilogue

*Three Years Later*

REESE STEPPED UP to his friends, handing over glasses of whisky as they stood around watching the horde of children racing around the grass.

"To number eight. Congratulations, Shay!" Reese tapped his glass to Shay's before tapping Finn's glass.

After the first sip, Shay held up his glass. "To number nine, may he or she arrive with health and happiness," he said in Finn's direction.

They both turned to Reese. "Should we expect number ten from you shortly to even up the number?"

"I'm pleased with the two we have. Remember we started later than you." He pointed to the squirming children playing with Belle. "Besides, we have more than enough between the lot of us." It turned out that his first child with Harlow had come expediently after their marriage. It was good they had both figured things out when they did or they would have found themselves forced into marriage after all.

"Aye. We've been blessed with fertility, that is for certain," Shay agreed.

"Not to mention the good luck to have had the most amazing lasses all but fall into our laps."

"You make it sound so easy," Finn said. "I almost left her

sitting there on the tavern steps. Only my conscience stopped me."

Shay huffed a laugh. "I nearly put Thea out on her ear when I found her in my home. I'm certainly glad I changed my mind and decided to keep her around." He shook his head. "I kept too many secrets."

"We all kept too many secrets," Reese agreed.

"But we've learned from our mistakes and have had good fortune since." After finishing their drinks and watching their wives seated in the shade for a few minutes, they seemed to have come to a silent agreement to give up their company for softer, more lovely attention.

Taking their daughter from his wife, Reese handed her over to his mother, the dowager, and took Harlow's hand to lead her to the beach for some time alone. The castle having been overrun with his friends and their families meant them having to find other places to spend time alone.

"Why did we invite everyone here?" he asked teasingly as they dashed away from a wave before he scooped her up into his arms.

"They only arrived yesterday afternoon and already you regret inviting them?"

"Can we ask them to leave tomorrow? I want our quiet, boring life back."

"Boring?" she chided.

"I would much rather spend our evenings reading the latest Stonecliff novel than having to play charades and listen to our children sing. I daresay, only our Luke can carry a tune."

"We have all our lives to spend together. Another day won't hurt."

"No. I suppose not," he agreed easily as he kissed her. He'd never been so lucky to have had this woman wash up on his beach and into his life. He'd never let her go.

THE END.

# ABOUT THE AUTHOR

One very early morning, Allison B. Hanson woke up with a conversation going on in her head. It wasn't so much a dream as being forced awake by her imagination. Unable to go back to sleep, she gave in, went to the computer, and began writing. Years later it still hasn't stopped.

Allison lives near Hershey, Pennsylvania and writes Highlander Historical and Scottish Regencies.

Catch up with Allison on any of her social media platforms here:

Website:
allisonbhanson.wordpress.com

Facebook:
facebook.com/BlueRidgeRomance

Twitter:
@AllisonBHanson

Instagram:
@allisonbhanson

Goodreads:
goodreads.com/author/show/9860589

BookBub:
bookbub.com/authors/allison-b-hanson